"Derek, the . . . . "
Amy s . . . .

She . . . . d
didn't v . . . .
ing on . . . .

He studied her for a moment before he spoke. "Amy, love, I think it's too late to go back. And the music has just begun."

Then, to the accompaniment of nothing but her heartbeat, he began to waltz.

There was a hushed murmur in the room as the two of them moved together, and soon the band took up the lush strains of "The Blue Danube" as Derek whirled Amy around the floor. Her gown flew around them, billowing like mauve waves, and the rest of the world was a blur. Only Derek's face remained in focus, smiling at her. His right palm pressed flat against the small of her back, sending eddies and flurries of tingles up her spine. All her senses were taken with him; even the full tempo of the waltz was part of him, echoing his masculine strength and his irresistible smile.

As the room swirled past, images flashed in and out of Amy's mind in triple time: Derek in his movie roles, Derek dancing with her, Derek leaning forward in the moonlight to kiss her . . .

She didn't believe in love at first sight, she silently asserted, lowering her head to avoid his piercing gaze. She was only responding to him physically, and who wouldn't? After all, she knew nothing of this man.

But that wasn't true. She knew more than she could consciously understand, because the heart always knows more than the mind. . . .

Bantam Books by Nancy Holder
Ask your bookseller for the titles you have missed

WINNER TAKE ALL
  (Loveswept #30)

THE GREATEST SHOW ON EARTH
  (Loveswept #47)

FINDERS KEEPERS
  (Loveswept #77)

OUT OF THIS WORLD
  (Loveswept #103)

HIS FAIR LADY
  (Loveswept #118)

WHAT ARE *LOVESWEPT* ROMANCES?

They are stories of true romance and touching emotion. We
believe those two very important ingredients are constants
in our highly sensual and very believable stories in the
LOVESWEPT line. Our goal is to give you, the reader,
stories of consistently high quality that may sometimes make
you laugh, sometimes make you cry, but are always fresh
and creative and contain many delightful surprises within
their pages.

Most romance fans read an enormous number of books.
Those they truly love, they keep. Others may be traded with
friends and soon forgotten. We hope that each *LOVESWEPT*
romance will be a treasure—a "keeper." We will always try
to publish

LOVE STORIES YOU'LL NEVER FORGET
BY AUTHORS YOU'LL ALWAYS REMEMBER

The Editors

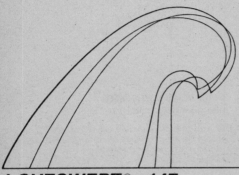

LOVESWEPT® · 147

Nancy Holder
Once in Love
With Amy

 BANTAM BOOKS
TORONTO · NEW YORK · LONDON · SYDNEY · AUCKLAND

ONCE IN LOVE WITH AMY
A Bantam Book / July 1986

LOVESWEPT® and the wave device are registered
trademarks of Bantam Books, Inc. Registered in U.S. Patent
and Trademark Office and elsewhere.

All rights reserved.
Copyright © 1986 by Nancy Holder.
Cover art copyright © 1986 by Bantam Books, Inc.
This book may not be reproduced in whole or in part, by
mimeograph or any other means, without permission.
For information address: Bantam Books, Inc.

ISBN 0-553-21751-8

Published simultaneously in the United States and Canada

Bantam Books are published by Bantam Books, Inc. Its
trademark, consisting of the words "Bantam Books" and
the portrayal of a rooster, is Registered in U.S. Patent and
Trademark Office and in other countries. Marca Registrada.
Bantam Books, Inc., 666 Fifth Avenue, New York, New
York 10103.

PRINTED IN THE UNITED STATES OF AMERICA

O   0 9 8 7 6 5 4 3 2 1

To all you little devils at Software Heaven,
and your loved ones too

One

Derek Morgan's heart was pounding. He imagined that every step he took in his squeaking Adidas sounded the alarm that would ruin him. He hesitated a moment on the deck of the *H.M.S. Princess Margaret*, his mind conjuring up bells and sirens and the shrill soprano of a dowager shouting, "Stop that man!" As he crept on, palms sweating, perspiration beading his high forehead, the breathtaking dread of discovery swirled around him like the fog.

He grinned. He was having a wonderful time.

For once, he found his height a disadvantage. Even hunched, he felt vulnerably obvious to any passerby, but he was grateful for his black hair, which blended into the shadows. The wavy curls hooded his head, so they looked like an extension of his black turtleneck sweater, camouflage for the night's wild work.

Squeak, squeak, squeak, cheeped his sneakers, sending a delicious thrill of anxiety up his spine.

Just one more yard, he told himself, *and feet, don't you fail me now.*

Stealthily he flexed one gloved hand and held it out as if to gauge his distance to the door of the darkened stateroom. In his other hand he fingered the passkey that would gain him easy entry. He frowned as he glanced upward: the massive cruise ship was outrunning the gauzy streaks of clouds that covered the moon. At any moment the light could flood the deck, exposing him.

He fervently prayed to the ghosts of all cat burglars now picking the locks of the Pearly Gates to protect him from being caught. Not too soon, oh, not yet—it was too early into the game and far too much fun.

At last he touched the doorknob. Derek tightened his fingers around it and smiled as he exhaled. The Committee was right: theft was addictive, particularly when you were successful at it . . . *and* being paid handsomely to do it, as well.

What a strange way to earn a living, he mused, but stranger things had happened to Derek Morgan, once a gangly lad from a small Welsh mining village and now the thirty-year-old toast of Los Angeles, New York, and other major cities of the world. Still, if anyone had told him he'd one day find himself on a summer crossing from New York to Southampton on a glamorous floating palace built in the heyday of Art Deco, preparing to break into someone's room, he'd have burst out with the famous Derek Morgan laugh.

But here he was! He *was* on a summer crossing, into the second of nine days, in fact; and this *was* the *Meg*, and as for breaking in, well, he'd best get on with it. He had a dinner engagement with one of the most charming women he'd ever met, and he didn't want to keep her waiting any longer than he had to.

"So, ye blackguard, do the dirty deed," he rasped to himself in a pirate's brogue. He inserted the skeleton key and opened the door. As he crept inside, the ship's huge foghorns let forth with a triumphant blare.

* * *

Amy van Teiler danced in the wind, her skirts flapping around her like mauve-and-jade butterfly wings. Throwing back her head, she watched the moon frolic with the clouds, playing hide-and-seek as it cast glowing beams on the shiny wooden deck of the *Princess Margaret.* Threads of silver and gold shot through the rushing water below and reflected back into her hair, which she had freed from the ballerina chignon at the nape of her neck. It flew behind her like streamers of bright yellow silk.

" 'Pussycat, pussycat, where have you been? I've been to London to see the Queen,' " she sang to the blustery night, hugging herself as she twirled in a circle. For she *was* going to London—if not to see Queen Elizabeth, then to begin a brand-new life.

Which, actually, had already begun. She looked down at her gown, a perfect replica of an Erte design from 1924, and giggled. Wouldn't Mrs. Bordon be happy when she saw her? Amy thought, adjusting the silver clasps of the single capelike sleeve of her crepe gown. Her left shoulder was bare, the diagonal bodice piped with mauve that was repeated in the lining of the sleeve. The clinging fabric molded the contours of her small, high breasts, then plummeted down her stomach to a woven sash belted just above her girlishly narrow hips. Silver drop earrings tangled with the riot of baby-fine hair tossed by the sea wind, exposing the classical oval of her face. She had thought to wear heavy makeup with the exotic ensemble, but she knew she couldn't carry it off. With her fine features, brown doe eyes, and cupid-bow lips, she would have looked like a little girl parading in her mother's dress. It wasn't her mother's dress she was wearing, though, but a copy of Mrs. Bordon's mother's dress.

Her employer, Geneva Bordon, was a woman after her own heart, indulging in fantasy and playing dress-up on a grand scale, bringing to life old times and old memories with a theatrical flourish. They had found each other through one of Amy's costume-design professors at San Diego State, but it was Amy's previous experience of traveling with the Renaissance fair, selling costumes and living the part of an Elizabethan lady, that had cinched her the job as Mrs. Bordon's theme-cruise designer.

Indulging in fantasy. Amy frowned. She had spent too much of her life doing that. She and her older sister, Claire, had joined the Renaissance troupe to escape Aunt Norma, who had been saddled with them when their parents died in a rafting accident. Aunt Norma had never wanted children, and certainly didn't want Claire and Amy—oh, she had made that clear, over and over again!—and so the two of them had run away to join the fair when Amy was only sixteen, an early graduate of high school. Claire, a decade older, continued in her role of mother substitute, striving to make up for Norma's cruelty and neglect. They had lived like Gypsies, avoiding life's problems by moving away from them until Claire had married. Then their fantasylike existence had vanished as quickly as the beauty of a glorious summer sunset. . . .

Next Claire had put Amy through college, and then through graduate school, too, when Amy, armed with only a B.A., hadn't been able to find work. Yet even with her master's degree, she hadn't seriously applied her talents to the business of making a living. Somehow she managed to keep postponing the cold, hard reality of self-reliance by remaining within the shelter of college life, helping her profs with their design shows and drama department plays; and knocking around the local drama scene, working on musicals and little theater productions.

But it was a hand-to-mouth existence, and she knew she could do better. She also knew that Claire worried about her and wanted her to become more responsible. There were always large gifts of cash at Christmas and on her birthdays—not that Claire disapproved of her, not at all. Still, it was time for Amy to stop playacting that she was a princess shielded from the grittiness of the world and buckle down to make something of herself.

So she was off to London, and the position of research assistant at London University. A plum of a job, if not exactly . . . exciting. She thought of dusty tomes and theoretical abstracts—why, the history of muslin alone filled volumes—and sighed absently.

But it was a steady job at last. A salary. A chance to make good use of the expensive education Claire had provided. Claire was so proud of Amy for landing the assistantship. Unlike Aunt Norma, Claire had always believed in her, fighting back when Norma told Amy she was stupid, no good, a burden. All her life, Claire had battled to help Amy get and keep her self-esteem, and she had always expected Amy to blossom. And that in itself was reason enough for Amy to accept the London position.

But she had no more time to ponder the future. It was chilly, and she was probably already late for dinner. The stewards had paraded up and down the corridors with their toylike glockenspiels ten minutes ago, sounding the call for the second seating of the evening.

And she needed to do something about her windswept hair, she remembered, smoothing it with her hands.

Her skirt fluttered against her shins as she walked toward the set of carved wooden doors that led to the dining room. Just as she reached them, she heard another door open a few yards to the right and idly turned her head in the direction of the sound.

A tall man dressed in a black turtleneck sweater, jeans, and gloves furtively tiptoed out. Feeling silly but unable to stop, Amy flattened herself against the bulkhead and watched him warily shut the door. The wind caught and whipped his ebony hair, lustrous in the moonlight. He looked in all directions, even above his head, and though the planes of his face were hidden by shadow, his eyes burned into the night as he turned and seemingly stared straight at her.

She held her breath. He hadn't caught sight of her standing there so foolishly. She tried to expel her breath but couldn't, because she was completely stunned by the sight of the man. He had moved away from the door, and his frame was backlit by the moon. He was incredible. Her eye, trained to the nuances of form and figure, noted the expanse of his shoulders, the masculine absence of waist, his small hips. The jeans outlined solid thighs; the sweater did the same to biceps and forearms. He had a long, slender neck for a man, made for the Irish sweaters of a mournful Gaelic poet; for the high-necked ruffled shirts of Heathcliff and Mr. Rochester; for the exquisite clothes of heroes from centuries gone by.

He stood still. So did she. Then he removed his gloves and stuffed them into a cloth bag. Slinging it over one magnificent shoulder, he turned on his heel and disappeared into the wind-tossed darkness.

Amy blinked. Had all that just happened? No, he was too handsome to be real. Her overactive imagination had invented him. He was just a mirage, brought on by the heady excitement of the cruise and her prospects in London.

But what a mirage. She sighed.

Then she spied something darting along the deck like a bird, tripping toward the sea. She moved forward, chased it a few feet, and picked it up.

It was a lady's fan. A scene of some sort was painted on the back, and the silken semicircle was edged in black lace.

Amy cocked her head at the closed stateroom door. Had it been a secret rendezvous between two ghosts, then? One a Spanish *señorita*, the other her pensive Irish poet?

Without realizing it, she waved the fan against her cheek, warm despite the blustery night air.

"Hey, you, whoever you are," she whispered to the shadows that had swallowed up the man, "what are you doing here? And who *are* you?"

Fifteen minutes later, in the dining room, Geneva Bordon tapped her sugar spoon against her champagne glass, calling her group to order. Everyone, including Amy, stopped chatting and looked at her expectantly.

"This is our second night together, everyone. Isn't it marvelous?"

Amy winced as Mrs. Bordon squeezed her hands together and pressed them against her chest, nearly crushing the spray of fresh violets pinned in the center of her exquisitely cut black velvet dinner dress. Violets were hard to come by on a cruise ship, and Amy had hoped to make them last for at least one more costume change. The gown was an adaptation of a creation by famed costume designer Travis Banton for Dorothy Lamour in 1937, and Lamour had actually worn the original to the Bordons' second-anniversary dinner in San Francisco that year—complete with violets.

"This is our first night in full dress," Mrs.

Bordon continued, "and I do hope you all get into the spirit of things. Picture yourselves back in the thirties, the glamour days of ships like this. I know your outfits will help. They were made, of course, by our own Amy van Teiler!"

Smiling shyly, Amy inclined her head. Their Italian waiter, Giovanni, smiled at her in a leering, Lothario sort of way. Across the table, Mrs. Bordon's nubile grandniece, Mara, gave him a quelling look. Immediately he moved to Mara's side and rearranged her silverware, and she favored him with a languorous sigh as he discreetly brushed his wrist against her forearm.

"I have an announcement to make," Mrs. Bordon went on. "Tonight we will be honored with a surprise dinner guest. No, not the captain—he's coming tomorrow! Our guest is going to be a little late, due to a previous engagement, and he's asked us to start without him. But you'll all be *so* pleased when he does arrive!"

Excited murmurings buzzed through the group. Mrs. Bordon's husband, Basil, whom she had never called anything but "Bobo" since the day she'd met him, patted her hand. "I'm glad you're having a good time, dear," he said. He looked like the little man on the cards in a Monopoly game, from his round face and bald pate to his bushy white moustache. "But please don't overexcite yourself."

Mrs. Bordon leaned forward, dodging the centerpiece of mums and asters on the table as she winked at Amy. "Overexcite myself. Humph. Amy, dear, do I appear overexcited?"

Amy couldn't help but grin. For all her seventy-one years, Geneva Bordon was as flushed and excited as a little girl. But then, Amy had never seen her otherwise.

"Look at her, Bobo," Mrs. Bordon said, reaching across the table to touch Amy's cheek. "Isn't she adorable? Oh, when I was young, I wanted so much to have shiny blond hair like yours, dear. And those big brown eyes, just like Loretta Young's! She looks like a bisque doll in her Erte gown, don't you agree?"

Mr. Bordon's face was hidden from Amy's view by the centerpiece, but she heard his patient and amused, "Yes, dear," and fought to keep down a giggle.

"Just like Mother." Mrs. Bordon looked past her husband to smile at her grandniece. "Mara, darling, did you know Amy's wearing a copy of the dress Mother wore to the dinner celebrating my tenth birthday?"

Mara looked singularly unimpressed. "Yes, Aunt Geneva. I know."

"Isn't it charming the way she went through all our old scrapbooks and sewed up all the clothes for our little soiree?"

Mara took a sip of wine. "Yes, Aunt Geneva. Simply charming." As she spoke, she tugged on the lace inset of her black satin gown—another van Teiler recreation—as if she wanted to display some more of her cleavage.

Of which there was plenty, Amy noted wistfully. The only word for Mara was voluptuous. While she wasn't fat, she'd amassed curves Amy could only sigh over.

"Tired, dear?" Mrs. Bordon asked.

Amy roused herself. "No, not in the least." She laughed. "I haven't done anything to be tired from."

"Nonsense. You did alterations all afternoon." She covered Amy's hand with her own. "We already agreed that the work you did before the cruise— making these lovely clothes—was worth your passage to England. I don't expect you to do anything else except to have fun."

"I want to make sure everyone's clothes fit," Amy insisted.

Mrs. Bordon patted Amy's wrist and shook her head wonderingly. "Such a worker! Don't you think, Mara?"

Yawning, Mara nodded.

"Well, you're not a servant, Amy. We're square, you and I, and I'll pay you for any extra work you do."

Amy looked horrified. "Mrs. B., no! I really want—"

"Look!" Mrs. Bordon interjected. "There's our mystery guest!" She clasped her hands against her chest again, hitting the violets dead center. "Mr. Derek Morgan!"

As if on cue, a man appeared under the etched-glass jamb across the room, his profile reflected a hundred times in a wall of glass on his right.

"Who?" Mr. Bordon queried, looking up from his toast rounds and caviar.

Amy gasped. Derek Morgan! Why hadn't she realized! He was the fan man, the heroic apparition! She touched her bare collarbone as if to recapture her heart's missed beat. Though he had changed into a tuxedo that must have been fitted inch by inch onto his body, there was no mistaking the wavy hair, the feline movements, the eyes.

"Bobo, dear, he's Britain's most popular actor," Mrs. Bordon explained, waving vigorously.

At last Amy could see his entire face, though of course she'd recently seen it stretched across the silver screen back home, in San Diego. Oh, the eyes. How could she not have recognized him! He'd played the lead in a remake of *Taras Bulba*, and it was perfect casting: His tanned features were rough, angular, barbaric. He had a high forehead, a long, straight nose, and a square chunk of jaw softened by full lips. A Cossack, surely, and not a civilized Englishman. She remembered the love scenes in the movie and a wave of heat rose like steam around her. Definitely not civilized.

Everyone in the dining room rose and applauded him; he hesitated, then jauntily waved at Mrs. Bordon as she hailed him again and began to press through the crowds to escort him back to the table.

"Mmm, what a body," Mara said beneath her breath. Giovanni scowled at her.

"Did you say something, pet?" Mr. Bordon asked, cupping his ear.

Mara demurely lowered her lashes. "No, Uncle Bobo."

They watched as Derek Morgan walked toward Mrs. Bordon, looking utterly charmed to see her.

"That man has a nice physique," Mr. Bordon commented, then went back to his caviar.

"Mr. Morgan!" Mrs. Bordon exclaimed, shaking Derek's hand vigorously. "I'm so happy you could make it this evening."

Her smile was one of pleasure, with only a little awe, and the way she so forthrightly gripped his fingers helped put Derek at ease.

"Thank you, Mrs. Bordon. I'm looking forward to it. I've been eating alone in my stateroom."

"Oh, pshaw! As if no one in this entire room hasn't tried to invite you to *something*."

"I've been keeping a low profile, actually," he drawled wryly, thinking of the successful crime he'd just committed. He was sorry his presence on board was now common knowledge; it would be harder to continue the break-ins, with people on the lookout for him. For that reason alone he'd tried—halfheartedly, he admitted—to persuade the Committee he was a bad choice for the job. But they'd been insistent. He hoped he wouldn't let them down.

"A low profile on a ship like this?" she countered, echoing his thoughts. "A famous man like you?"

"Fame is new to me, Mrs. Bordon. I struggled for twelve years to become an 'overnight sensation.' " And struggled was the word.

"A modest man. I wasn't sure they made them anymore. Imagine, all that and your beautiful accent too! I couldn't have designed you better if I'd made you up myself." She chuckled. "It's just like a movie."

He grinned at the top of her head as they wove their way around huge gold-trimmed columns fluted with lotus blossoms and tables surrounded by shining faces, kept at bay by the fierce look of the maître d'. Mrs. Bordon certainly was an excitable woman, so filled with goodwill, Derek could feel it. If he didn't watch out, she would adopt him.

His grin grew when he caught sight of the costumed members of her party. The women were clad in remakes of movie stars' dinner dresses from films he'd watched on late-night telly, and the men sported pleated trousers and fobs. As a Britisher he prized eccentricity—as an actor he lived it—and Mrs. Bordon ranked up there with Britain's finest.

The grin automatically transformed into the famous Derek Morgan smile when he noticed the brunette standing next to an empty chair. Oh, let it be his, he thought. She was fabulously overdone, with a stunning chest displayed to advantage in a low-cut black lace number. She had strong, almost harsh, features—an eighties Joan Crawford, he decided, his interest growing. She stared right at him, unabashed, and he chuckled aloud when he caught the flash of irritation on the face of the waiter standing beside her. Derek saw at once there'd been a little something going on between them. He knew cruise waiters and he knew flashy brunettes, many of them intimately—the brunettes, not the waiters—and he sighed in anticipation of the long siege of seduction that dinner was about to become.

They reached the head table. Derek moved down it like a reception line of one, shaking hands with these curious reflections from the past, startled to have one elderly woman curtsy to him as if he were a member of the Royal Family.

". . . my cousin, Mildred Hopkins," Mrs. Bordon was saying, "and this is Geronimo Jones, who does the pool maintenance at our Santa Barbara home. He's still a hippie, can you imagine?"

Derek was cordial as she introduced each person, but impatient to reach the brunette. "How do you do?" he said to the wizened, white-bearded Geronimo, who wore a beaded headband with his Fred Astaire white tie and tails.

"Now, I thought I'd seat you across from my niece, Mara Northcoate, and next to my—well, what are you, Amy, love?"

Her niece, Derek thought, still smiling as he shook the brunette's hand. Drat. That could make things awkward.

"I'm your sewing lady," said a crystal-bright voice behind him. The clarity of it startled him, and he turned.

He was startled for a second time. Words flooded his mind as he looked at the small woman with yellow-blond hair: pretty, petite, lovely, so, well . . . *enchanting.*

Her lips parted when he looked at her, and her brown eyes grew as large as film cans. He had to fight an insane urge to put his arms around her and tell her not to be nervous.

"I'm Pleased van Teiler," she blurted out. "I'm Amy to meet you."

They shook hands. Lightning struck, once, twice, three times, and Derek stood rooted to the spot, galvanized by the sensations that were sparking through his fingers and arm. His response to her was instantaneous and over-whelming. It seemed he stared at her for hours, though he knew that couldn't be, for he had stopped breathing.

Where have you been? he asked her silently, overwhelmed by his intense reaction to her. What was happening to him?

"I'm Amy . . ." she said again.

"Likewise," he murmured.

Two

Derek was jerked to an awareness of what they were saying by a titter from Mara: *I'm Amy to meet you. Likewise, I'm sure.* Mara was a brittle lady, somewhat unkind, thinking nothing of anyone's feelings but her own. In short, his type. While Pleased was obviously very sweet, very open, very . . . vulnerable. A fairy princess, a spun-sugar girl.

With lightning in her fingers. He stared down at their clasped hands and gingerly broke contact.

He felt his composure returning. The successful theft must have stimulated him more than he'd realized: here he was acting like a love-struck teenager!

And there she stood, completely oblivious to the staggering power she'd unleashed on him. Unbelievable.

Derek Morgan was a man who assessed his options quickly. Best to stay away from her, his conscience advised. The fragile, magical Miss van Teiler was not for the womanizing likes of him.

"You'll be just a little cramped, since we've had to put in an extra place," Mrs. Bordon said, leading him around to Amy's side of the table and gesturing for the sulking Giovanni to pull out Derek's chair. "I do hope you won't mind."

"No, not at all." He squeezed into his place, brushing Amy's thigh with his own. Not looking at him, she flushed and picked up her water glass.

"Will *you* be comfortable?" he asked her.

Turning redder still, she nodded. Mrs. Bordon patted her on the top of her head and walked back around the table.

Immediately a white china plate of caviar, toast, and trimmings was placed before him. Accomplished servants, two more waiters silently appeared to fill his champagne, water, and other wineglasses, then withdrew.

"So here we are," Mrs. Bordon said, giggling sheepishly. "I told you about my cruise during shuffleboard this afternoon, Mr. Morgan. What do you think?"

He grinned. "I think it's smashing."

"Do you think I'm silly, trying to relive my youth?" Before he could reply, she sighed and went on. "I adore the *Princess Margaret* almost as much as I adore life, which is almost as much as I adore my husband." She beamed at Bobo. "I've crossed the ocean many times on this grand old lady. They still have the same registry in the chapel that we signed when we got married on board," she added, her lined cheeks rosy.

"Nineteen thirty-five," Mr. Bordon put in.

"Yes, dear," Mrs. Bordon murmured lovingly. "Our signatures are faded now. We're going to renew our vows on the last night."

She slumped. "Oh, I just can't believe this is the *Meg*'s last voyage! In seven more days she'll never sail again. *Never.* That's why I need to bid her a grand farewell."

"It's going to be made into a floating hotel, Aunt Geneva," Mara said impatiently. "You can still stay on it whenever you want."

Beside Derek, Amy's eyes flashed. "But it won't be the same!"

Derek smiled at her, intrigued by the fire that blazed beneath her placid surface. But she was still looking at Mara.

Mrs. Bordon held out her hands. "That's right. It won't be the same at all. Oh, if only you young people could have lived in my day . . . the days I'm trying to recreate, like a silly old goose. Things were so much more glamorous . . . so *romantic.*"

Derek turned his gaze on the elderly lady. "These are still your days, madam," he said softly.

Mrs. Bordon's mouth dropped open, and Derek heard Amy's quick intake of breath. "What a lovely thing to say!" Mrs. Bordon cried. "Oh, Bobo, wasn't it lovely?"

Basil Bordon smiled at her. "Yes, my dear. My very thoughts, as well."

"It's true," Derek insisted. Across from him, Mara narrowed her eyes in a cynical, hooded expression that told him she assumed he was simply turning on the charm to flatter her great-aunt.

"But tell me, Derek," Mrs. Bordon pressed. "Do you think my cruise party is foolish? I thought it would be fun to invite a few friends and transport everybody back to the 'good old days' for the *Meg*'s last crossing."

"I think it's a wonderful idea." Derek didn't find it necessary to mention that in the "good old days" of the late thirties, his father was a child-laborer slaving in a coal mine and glad for the work; that his uncle had contracted polio; that in their little village babies had starved.

He was the son and grandson of men who had toiled long in the mines and had little to show for it. As a boy, he had dreamed of escaping the dreary, gray village and the trap it represented. He had imagined himself a hero, saving his family from the black lung and the creditors . . . and ultimately his imagination had saved them all. He was being touted as the new Laurence Olivier and the acting jobs were at last rolling in. Mum, a widow now, lived in luxury in London, and his brothers and sisters had bright hopes and futures of their own.

A hero . . . he made his living playing the hero.

And the thief, for the time being.

"Thank you for understanding my little flight of fancy," Mrs. Bordon said, interrupting his musing. "I simply couldn't have achieved the proper effect without Amy, though. She's a treasure."

"I don't doubt that." Derek glanced at Amy, and her face drained of color. There was an aura of defenselessness about her that made him feel like a barbarian when he just looked at her. He couldn't help his appraising sweep of her body—it was second nature to him—but she didn't revel in it, as Mara Northcoate did. But then, Mara was already his for the taking. She was anyone's.

But Pleased van Teiler? Though he guessed she was in her mid-twenties, he wondered if anyone had ever had her. The way her luminous brown eyes dilated when he looked too long, the surprised O of her Kewpie-doll mouth—they made her seem virginal compared to Mara's vampish overtures. Why, right now Mara was pressing on his instep with her shoe, demanding some attention. And the waiter looked as if he'd like to drop cyanide in Derek's Dom Perignon.

Amy met his gaze, apparently innocent of the impact of her gigantic eyes, soft as velvet, rich as chocolate. "I—uh, I believe we've met before," she said brashly, and he registered his surprise that she would use such a trite line on him.

"No, I mean, really." She reached for her wineglass and looked disappointed to see it empty.

Gallantly he offered her his as another slow smile

crossed his lips. He suddenly felt boyish, and not the jaded movie star everyone—including himself—supposed he was. She was extraordinary. He hadn't been intrigued like this by anyone for a long time.

A long time? Whom did he think he was kidding? He had *never* been this intrigued by a woman in his life. Including Cecily . . .

"I think so too," he said softly, raising his champagne goblet and studying her, enjoying himself. "On a wild moor, perhaps, or in the court of a king."

"Surely you're not talking about reincarnation," Mara said scoffingly.

He shrugged. "Why not? Don't you believe in soul mates?"

Beneath the intensity of his look, Mara blanched. Mrs. Bordon held up a cautioning hand and murmured, "My niece is recovering from a recent divorce, Mr. Morgan."

One of a long string of them, Derek guessed, and inclined his head. "Pardon me. I hope I haven't offended you." In reply Mara pressed a now-bare foot against his shin.

"Not at all," she said aloud.

"You know, we met Amy at a Renaissance fair in San Diego," Mrs. Bordon put in, apparently trying to smooth things over. "She used to travel all over the country with her sister. You should see her in her royal court costume." She bobbed her white head at Mara. "*Then* you'd believe in reincarnation. She looked as if she'd stepped from the pages of a history book." She laughed and turned to Derek. "As she does now. She's wearing a copy of the dress my mother wore to the dinner celebrating my tenth birthday. Isn't that charming?"

Amy managed a weak smile that melted his heart. "Very charming," Derek concurred.

"She made all the costumes you see around you! She's so clever!"

"Indeed," Derek said.

"She's going to start a new job at London University as a design research associate. Oh, look how she blushes at the mention! It's her most cherished dream, to live in England."

Derek laughed. "Mine too. I'm there so seldom."

"You know, I haven't the vaguest idea how people make movies," Mara cut in petulantly, obviously wanting to be Derek's focus of attention. "I'd love to hear about some of your experiences, Derek."

Amy heard Derek Morgan stifle a sigh before he said, "As you wish." He must get tired of talking about himself, she thought. While all this attention was flattering, it must also get wearing.

She should know. She'd only had a few moments of attention from him and she was exhausted. And acting like a nitwit, she knew, but she couldn't help it.

It wasn't just that he was a show-business superstar, though that in itself was daunting. No, it was something far more . . . elemental. There was a physical force reaching out from him, a vital current, an electricity, that completely mesmerized her. When he looked at her, she forgot how to talk. How to think. All she could do was feel that energy engulfing her, consuming her, spilling into her being and filling her with a strange dizziness that made the room tilt and her heart pound as though it were going to burst. It was the most bizarre sensation she had ever experienced.

It was also the most wonderful.

People in the Renaissance believed in love at first sight, she mused, shifting slightly as plates were changed and more food was put in front of her. Oh, but that was silly. What she was feeling was the furthest thing from love. It was pure, unadulterated star-worship, which must afflict millions of

women who palpitated over the devastating pul-
chritude of Derek Morgan. Love at first sight
indeed. Her overactive imagination, more like.

The conversation swirled around her; she
couldn't make sense any longer of anything anyone
was saying. She felt disoriented, like a dreamer
aware she was dreaming and struggling to wake
up.

Another change of plates occurred.

They believed love affected you physically, she
pondered, that falling instantly in love was not
only possible, but happened quite often. . . .

"Miss van Teiler?" Derek queried.

She roused herself, eyes widening when she saw
that she was eating a French pastry. Good grief,
she'd missed the entire meal! She must have sat
there for an hour in paralyzed silence, mechanically eating while Derek and the others talked. She
couldn't believe it.

"Yes?" Her voice was hoarse. From lack of use,
she thought glumly.

"I asked if you wanted to dance."

Before she could answer, he rose from his chair
and pulled out hers. She caught a whiff of sandalwood and thought it must be his after-shave.
Somehow it had hypnotized her.

Or his eyes had done it, or his smile . . .

Then his hand was cupping her bare shoulder as
she stood, his long, strong fingers burning her
skin. Amy swallowed, heat rising up her neck
when she saw the look on Mr. Bordon's face. It was
the radiant triumph of a matchmaker who had
scored. Two faces down, Mara peevishly stabbed
her chocolate eclair and Giovanni smiled at Amy as
he readjusted a white cloth over his arm.

Placing a firm but gentle hand under Amy's
elbow, Derek guided her to the wooden dance floor.
His fingertips were like satin.

Only a few couples were dancing. At one end of

the football field of wood, the ship's band reigned on a dais, and behind the group rose an enormous gold-and-silver lacquered mural filled with flying birds and sea horses and water maidens. In the center, a dazzling sun radiated a glowing brilliance.

"That's you," Derek said, smiling down on her. "Lady Sunshine."

He towered over her. If not for the careful way he held her, she would have gotten lost in his embrace, in the overpowering response her body made to his nearness. Gooseflesh rose on her arms and chest as if she were freezing, and yet she felt feverish. The merest brush of his skin against any part of her, even her gown, was like a sensuous caress against bare flesh.

How she began to dance with him she had no idea. Perhaps his self-assurance was enough for both of them. He moved easily, like Astaire, a man who could make any partner flow like Ginger Rogers.

No, *he* was the sun, she wanted to tell him, bravely lifting her face to bask in the golden rays of his look; but instead she managed a crooked smile and said, "Your line's worse than my line."

"But it wasn't a line," he protested, lowering his head to gaze more intently at her. His eyes were like polished onyx, shiny and nearly black, their depths textured by soft lights from twin banks of chandeliers. Gold flecks danced deep inside them, speaking of more gold within—of his soul.

"I'm sorry if I ignored you at dinner," she said, trying another tack to dissolve the power of his spell. "I was distracted . . . I mean, I was thinking about someone. Something."

"But you didn't ignore me." The corners of his mouth twitched. "You stared at me. It was very flattering."

She sighed. "Well, you've got to admit you're something to look at."

Chuckling, he touched her cheek. "So are you."

"Not like you. Nobody's eaten an entire meal without tasting it on *my* account."

His smile faded and his grip tightened on her hand, pulling her toward him. Her breasts were a whisper away from his hard chest. Though he smiled, she saw a hunger beneath his debonair charm. "Wrong," he said, his voice low and husky, rumbling through his rib cage. "So wrong."

She felt dizzy again. Shaking her head, her hand trembling in his grasp, she straightened and said, "I'm the kind of person doting old ladies pat on the head. In case you haven't noticed."

"I'm sure Mrs. Bordon would like to pat my head too. If she could reach it," he riposted, and they both smiled. "In fact, I'm waiting for her to adopt me." They chuckled in unison. "You see? I'm not so bad."

No. He was too good, she thought with a twinge of regret that she hadn't allowed him to hold her against his body. He was like a dream, a fantasy hero, and not a real man. She told herself she was reacting to the image that publicity departments and clever agents had invented—as well as her own imaginings when she had seen him step from the darkness into the moonlight. The romantic lover of the lady with the fan . . .

"We should be waltzing," he whispered. "The lost days of romance—that's what Geneva wants, isn't it? On a night like this, here, a man and a woman should lose themselves in the dance."

"Mr. Morgan . . ."

"Derek."

The music ended. The other couples, who had stopped dancing to watch Derek and Amy, applauded and smiled.

"Derek, the music's over. Let's go back," she said

breathlessly. She had begun to tremble in his arms, and she didn't want him to know the effect he was having on her. She was embarrassed and exhilarated at the same time, and very, very wary. This man was obviously a ladies' man, and she, while a lady, was not in the same league as he.

"Please."

He studied her for a moment before he spoke. "Amy, love, I think it's too late to go back. And the music has just begun."

Then, to the accompaniment of nothing but her heartbeat, he began to waltz.

There was a hushed murmur of appreciation in the room as the two of them moved together. The band took up the lush strains of the "Blue Danube" as Derek whirled Amy around the floor. Her gown flew around them, billowing like mauve waves, and the rest of the world was a blur. Only Derek's face remained focused, smiling at her, reveling in the lightning pace of the dance as he dipped and guided her with the grace of a dashing Viennese nobleman. His right palm pressed flat against the small of her back in a formal posture, sending eddies and flurries of tingles up her back that gathered inside her outstretched hand. She smelled his musky scent, a potent contrast to her own light floral cologne. All her senses were taken up with him—even the full tempo of the waltz was part of him, singing of his masculinity and his irresistible smile.

As the room cascaded past, images flashed in and out of Amy's mind in triple time, to the rhythm of the tension growing inside her: Derek in his movie roles; Derek with her, dancing as they were now; Derek leaning forward in the moonlight to kiss her; coming toward her, coming for her . . .

She didn't believe in love at first sight, she silently asserted, lowering her head to avoid his piercing gaze. She didn't, she didn't. She was only responding to him physically—who wouldn't? After all, she knew nothing of this man. Nothing.

But that wasn't true. She knew more than she could consciously understand, because the heart always knows more than the mind. . . .

The band ended the waltz with a flourish. Derek stopped. Standing stock-still with her in dance position, he stared at her wonderingly and said, "Thank you, Lady Sunshine."

All around them, the others were applauding their waltz; here and there, women touched handkerchiefs to their eyes.

It had been a most romantic gesture. And like a romantic hero, Derek's hair was carelessly tousled. The unruly curls of ebony reminded her of how he had looked in the love scenes in *Taras Bulba*. Fierce and sweating, making love with abandon, like an animal. She shut her eyes for a moment, a sudden rush of desire making her sway.

"Did I step on your foot?" Derek asked solicitously.

She shook her head. "I . . . I'm having a little trouble here," she confessed. "I, uh, you . . ."

"Yes, angel?" His voice was sonorous and kind, interested in her plight.

She drummed her fingers on his shoulder, realized what she was doing, and stopped. "Nothing. It's nothing. Thank you for the dance. It was— Geneva must have loved it."

She started to walk away. Derek grabbed her hand. "I didn't do it for Geneva. I did it for you . . . and me."

She couldn't quite look at him. "Oh."

He glanced down at their hands, then at her face. "I'm having a little trouble here too. It's impossible to get to know someone when everybody's staring. What do you say we go somewhere else? To a bar, perhaps, or . . ." He hesitated, his eyelids drooping over his golden irises. "My stateroom."

Amy was speechless. He was trying to pick her up. She was flattered, horrified, and about ready to say yes before she came to her senses and fainted dead away. Through a miracle, she managed to stay poised and simply shake her head.

Looking disappointed, he shrugged. "To a bar, then. I'd like some privacy with you. We can just talk, Amy, if you like. I need to be alone with you." His dark eyes gleamed. "I can't explain it. There's just this need . . ."

She cleared her throat. "Which 'need' is that?"

"I'm not talking about lust," he insisted, running his free hand through his hair, unknowingly smoothing the unruliness she'd found so enticing. "Well, I am, but not lust exclusively. There's something about you . . ."

"Can we go back to the table?" she asked hopefully, straining not to listen to, or believe, his melting words. The knights in shining armor she'd created in her fantasies paled in comparison to him and the things he was saying! She supposed she should simply laugh at him. Men didn't really talk like that. At least, none of the men she had ever known.

His heavy brows rose, accentuating the deep-set quality of his eyes. "I really frighten you, don't I? Why?"

"Oh, come on." She tried to slip her hand out of his grasp, but he squeezed more tightly.

"Why?" he repeated.

"Please, you're embarrassing me." When he wouldn't relent, she tilted her head and said, "For one thing, you're very famous. I'm not used to meeting celebrities."

He inclined his head. "I can't argue with that. And for another thing?"

"We already went into that," she muttered, looking away. "You're . . . good-looking."

"And that frightens you?" He smiled pleasantly.

"You're making this very difficult."

"Good."

She blew tendrils of hair away from her forehead. "Do you always toy with your dance partners?"

"Usually. But I'm not toying with you now, Amy. I'm not trifling with you and I'm not merely flirting. I'm honestly interested in you."

Her face burned as if the skin were scorched. "Please stop. Don't say anything more." She stared down at his hand, earnestly gripping hers. "And please let go of me."

"Amy, I want to—"

Just then Mara sashayed toward them and tapped Derek on the shoulder. "May I cut in?"

Derek hesitated long enough for Amy to step away from him and yield her place to Mara before he could answer for himself. "Have a nice time," she mumbled, grateful for the chance to escape—or was she grateful?—but piqued that Mara would be the means. Did that woman collect every man in sight? Or just the good-looking, dark ones?

Mara gave Amy a derisive once-over, then smiled up at Derek. "Oh, I intend to have a marvelous time. Shall we?"

Derek gazed past Mara to Amy, frustration and entreaty in his eyes. "Yes, of course. I'd be delighted."

He didn't sound delighted. Amy didn't want to take comfort in that, but did, as she walked back to their table.

Giovanni jerked her chair out with a brusque snap, then asked, "A brandy, *signorina*?" as if to make up for his lapse in good manners.

"Yes, thanks," Amy said on a long-drawn-out breath as she lowered herself into her seat.

Across from her, Mrs. Bordon beamed like a lighthouse. "Oh, my dear, that was so thrilling!

Don't you think, Bobo? The way they danced, at first without any music? So romantic!"

Mr. Bordon smiled patiently at his wife. "Quite so, my dear."

"Ah, shipboard kisses. Do you know, Amy, that once I was kissed by none other than Errol Flynn himself? It was on a short cruise from Maui to Oahu. So exciting! Although Bobo has him surpassed."

"My dear," Mr. Bordon reproved gently.

"Well, it's only the truth, Bobo! But to kiss Captain Blood himself . . ." She raised her eyes toward heaven. "It was an impetuous moment of whimsy. I knew it then too. But in the morning the steward brought me orchids. Dozens of them, in silver baskets. My clothes smelled of orchids for days."

The waiter placed a brandy snifter in front of Amy. As she picked it up, Geneva trilled, "A toast! Here's to romance! Here's to a beau for both my lovely girls!" She waved her glass in the direction of the dance floor, but abruptly her smile slipped. "Oh, dear, Bobo, they're dancing awfully close, don't you think?"

Amy looked over her shoulder. Derek and Mara appeared from within the crowd, coiled around each other—no formal waltzing for Mara!—and Amy quickly took another sip of brandy. Her disappointment embarrassed her far more than his flowery speeches had. She felt foolish for having put so much stock in his words and looks—like a lovesick movie fan, hanging onto his every syllable and twisting his words into things he hadn't said, or at least meant. Already he'd moved on to more promising territory.

"Times have changed, dear," Mr. Bordon said calmly. "Young people dance differently nowadays."

"Not *that* differently." Mrs. Bordon made a face. "I should have remembered that man's reputation. He really is a . . . an adventurous type, I've heard."

Covering her cheek with her hand, she made a moue of apology at Amy. "Silly me, throwing my lambs to a lion. Other than his . . . wildness, he's just the type for a fleeting moment on the *Meg*. Tall, dark, handsome, with an air of mystery around him."

Oh, yes, mystery, Amy thought, remembering the lace-edged fan. Maybe she should keep it as a souvenir of her dance with him—her brush with a fantasy in the flesh.

"And then there's his lovely accent," Mrs. Bordon went on. "Men with accents are intriguing."

Giovanni smiled.

"Errol Flynn had an accent too. He was Tasmanian, did you know? But in those days, a *good* girl was safe, even with that rake."

She sighed. "But oh, the joys of shipboard romance. There's nothing like it. One has a few days, a week if one is lucky. It all happens so fast, there's no chance for it to be less than perfect! One look, one glance, and you're madly in love—for a week!" She chuckled. "It's so heady, so divinely mad—but not to be taken seriously. It's simply to be enjoyed. Am I right, Bobo?"

"Entirely correct, my dear."

"But I don't suppose it's the same anymore. All this meeting in bars and jumping into bed. And the *movies*! My heavens, all that sex!"

Amy thought of Derek's steamy love scenes and took another sip of brandy.

"I wonder if it's even possible to indulge in a flirtation anymore."

"Sure it is," Mara drawled behind them, her arm threaded through Derek's.

"Well, hello, you two," Mrs. Bordon said brightly, indicating their chairs.

Mara reluctantly sat down, following Derek's progress to Amy's side of the table with a possessive air. "Is that brandy?" she asked, indicating her aunt's glass.

"Yes." She held up a finger, and Giovanni bobbed his head.

"And for the *signore*?" the waiter asked coldly.

"*Amaretto, per favore*," Derek requested, his Italian accent flawless.

"Not one accent, but two," Mrs. Bordon said archly.

"I beg your pardon?" Derek asked.

"Nothing. But tell me, Mr. Morgan—if you would indulge an old lady for a moment—do you believe in romance?"

Though he didn't look at her, Amy felt his attention shift in her direction. A warmth was born at the base of her spine and spiraled upward.

He grinned wolfishly at Mrs. Bordon. "Yes, of course I do."

Mrs. Bordon smiled. "Of course you do. Any man who can waltz as you do has to."

He half-stood. "Would you like . . .?"

She touched her chest. "Good heavens, no! I'm too old. But thank you. You're very chivalrous."

"Frankly, that's not a word used to describe me very often," he replied.

Mrs. Bordon nodded to herself. "Yes, I know. Pity, too."

Derek looked confused. Then he smiled an utterly charming, calculating smile at Mrs. Bordon. Pouring on the charm again, Amy thought. He didn't miss a trick.

"Would you mind if I borrowed Amy for a while?" he asked Mrs. Bordon. "There's a display of wax figures downstairs she promised to show me. Seems they're wearing very interesting costumes."

Amy's mouth dropped open. Mrs. Bordon, working her lips in a small gesture of concern, shrugged her shoulders and said, "Amy doesn't need my permission to do anything. We're all finished for the night."

"But you'll need help undressing," Amy said quickly.

Mrs. Bordon's blue eyes twinkled. "Bobo will help me," she drawled, thoroughly enjoying her own cheekiness.

"Oh, of course," Amy murmured.

Mara started to rise. "Well, I'd love to see—"

"If you'll excuse us," Derek interjected, rising. "Come on, Amy. It will close soon."

With a firm hold on her arm, he led Amy out of the grand dining room. Murmurs followed in their wake—*Look! She's leaving with Derek Morgan!*—and Amy fought the urge to duck her head. She wasn't used to having everyone staring at her. But Derek took it in stride.

Outside, she pulled herself away from him. "Why did you lie to her?"

He held out his hands. "To steal you away, of course."

She kept her distance, straining to ignore the rapid beating of her heart. Surely he could hear it. "I'd have thought you'd rather steal Mara."

He stood akimbo, smiling faintly as if he were enjoying her vexation. "Oho, you think I'm a superficial lout, don't you?"

"No." Those eyes of his—how did one keep from falling into them? "I just think you . . . you're like Errol Flynn," she finished lamely.

"The dark-haired rogue? And you prefer blonds?" He tweaked her earring with his forefinger. "I know I do."

The foghorns blared into the night, startling them both. Giving a little cry, Amy took an involuntary step toward Derek. Realizing the consequence of what she was doing, she tried to stop herself. She tottered on her silver leather high heels, reluctantly grasping his wrist as he steadied her by molding his large hand around her waist.

"Thanks," she said, and then, as his hand tightened, "Oh, oh, no . . ."

The moon beamed directly overhead, casting an aura of shimmering light around him. A bank of fog rose, swirling around him like a cloak as it lay across his broad shoulders, and through it his eyes burned into her, telling her of his desire for her, for little Amy van Teiler, the girl among women, the odd one out in her sister's life, for Cinderella. . . .

He turned the full force of his eyes on her, those gold-chased storms of jet, those Rasputin eyes that made her throat grow tight and her fingers clutch at him involuntarily. Soft fingertips spanned across the nape of her neck as he lowered his head to look at her, so tall she had to lift her chin to meet his gaze. And she had to look; though she tried to break contact, to repossess herself, his eyes wouldn't let her. They forced her to submit to his arms around her, his hard chest crushing her small, soft breasts, as his lips came nearer, nearer . . .

Her entire field of vision was filled with his eyes. His breath was scorching against her lips, his body heat burning her everywhere. Though her dress bared only one arm and shoulder, she felt naked and defenseless. She wanted to flatten her palms against his chest and push him away, but she couldn't move. She could only stare at him wonderingly.

"Amy, you're so beautiful," he said on a sigh, and his right hand slid from her waist and curved around her hip.

She gasped. Her loins seized; unimaginable sensations centered there like a golden sun, its rays shimmering across her breasts and downward into her abdomen. She saw the gold gleaming in his eyes, comet-hot. She gasped and arched herself against him, unaware of her intense response until he moaned softly in his throat and began to glide his hand up her side, following the indentation of her waist, the delicate ridges of her rib cage.

"Nooo." She groaned as Derek reached the roundness of the side of her breast. Ignoring her protest, he turned his hand sideways, fingertips pressing behind her arm as the heel of his hand rolled over the firm flesh of her feminine beauty, missing the contracting point that craved his touch. Then he cupped her under the arm with a gentle pressure, struggling to restrain himself. He moved as if in slow motion, as if sure the spell wouldn't break, implacable as a tide sweeping over her shoulder, across her chest, up the side of her neck.

"Oh, Mistress Pleased," he whispered, lodging his thumb beneath her chin and fanning his fingers behind her ear. He held her head in both hands as if it were a priceless work of art. His magical eyes shone and his lips parted, and his lids fell like swooping raven's wings as he bent to kiss her.

Mouth on mouth; the softness of his lips overwhelmed her more than a fiercer assault would have done. He brushed them over hers almost reverently, dissolving her fear and hesitation, sinking once more into a light-headed reverie. Falling, falling, then flying, as he parted her mouth and touched the tip of her tongue with his.

Ah! her body cried. Was the night on fire? Were his hands branding her? Was his tongue searing her soul?

He penetrated more deeply, exhaling through his nose against her upper lip. His tongue dueled with hers, seeking and finding the most sensitive places in her mouth. She jerked, and he held her, running his hand up and down the alabaster column of her neck and the pulse below her jaw, fanning the fire, raising the flames.

"Amy, I want you. My Lord, I want you. Let me make love to you, sweeting. Come with me to my stateroom."

With his words, both the fog and the spell lifted. Catching her breath, Amy broke away from him. She was being idiotic. Had she already forgotten her mortification in the dining room? How he had moved on to Mara? That he was an accomplished actor, a superstar famed for his many women, and she an incredibly hopeless romantic?

"Good night," she whispered, turning on her heel and forcing his hand to fall away from her body.

"Good night?" he repeated. "But Amy—"

"Good night, Errol Flynn!" she called.

"What? Wait! Come back!"

She didn't go back. She flew like the wind.

Three

He strode along the battlements, her hero, her
lord, clad in his iron armor, his plumed helmet
under his arm. Her crimson scarf was wrapped
around his biceps, and its tassels waved in the
searing wind. Scarlet flames shot up all around
him, nearly engulfing him as he swung his
broadsword at the enemy soldier clambering up
a ladder.

She covered her mouth but did not cry out as
she watched from the turret. She was a knight's
lady, and she must be fearless even when he was
in great peril. He was the people's champion, and
she must show her faith in him, to declare with
confidence that she knew he would vanquish
their foes and restore right to the land.

He cut down the intruder, then called for the
archers to load their bows. Oh, the ringing tones
of his manly voice! And how like a king he bore
himself! How nobly! The other warriors paled in
comparison, diminished by his glowing presence. Some of them trembled and cursed like
common men, showing their fear, but her lord
never wavered. If Milord Death rushed at him

35

that day. He would be met by a steadfast soul who would fight Him like one of His own demons.

Hours passed, smoke-blackened and filled with the cries of the wounded and the terrified. She swayed with exhaustion—she who had only stood and watched, while he had fought unceasingly, a lion among men!

And then it was ended. He stood with his head bowed for a moment in a prayer of thanksgiving, and her heart joined his. Then he unwrapped her scarf from around his arm and kissed it.

She left her place in the turret, flying down the stone steps to the great hall below, then through the smoldering embers and the running blood. Her flaxen hair whipped behind her as a rapturous smile played on her lips. Soon, soon, she would be in the arms of her beloved! He was the hero, and she was his lady!

Then her smile faded. Her heart turned to ashes.

Below her on the green, he stood with a tall, dark-haired woman whose ebony kirtle clung to high breasts and wide hips. The woman handed him a fan, and he kissed it. Then he drew the brazen wench into his mighty arms and kissed her, utterly forsaking his golden-haired lady!

With a cry of grief, she flung herself off the battlement, plunging down, down, down to her doom. . . .

Amy sat bolt upright in bed. "Derek!" she cried, and then the realization that she'd been dreaming flooded through her.

"Oh, for heaven's sake," she mumbled, red-cheeked, and lay back down. Images from the dream danced and faded, and she drew the crisp, cool sheets up to her neck, as if hiding from someone.

Which she was—or would be, come tomorrow. There was no way she was going to let Mr. Superstar Morgan practice his wily charm on her again. She was easy prey for such a man, and if she hadn't known that before, the dream had proved it. Lords and ladies, indeed! She was acting like a teenager!

Or rather, dreaming like one.

She tossed for half an hour, sighing deeply whenever she tried a new position in hopes of lulling herself to sleep. But each time she closed her eyes, she saw Derek as he had appeared in her dream, massive in his armor, and she would become so flustered she'd sigh and thrash into yet another position.

Finally she swung her legs over the side of the bed and ran her hands through her hair. "You're star-struck, you know that?" she chided her reflection in the circular mirror above her dressing table. "Next thing you know, you'll be asking him for an autographed picture to put under your pillow."

She stood, reaching for a cable-knit sweater and pleated trousers like Garbo's. "Let's walk it off, van Teiler," she ordered herself, and added a shawl to her ensemble to ward off the cold.

Derek waited two hours after Amy ran away from him before he broke into another stateroom. Now, as he stood in the center of the room, he frowned as he shined the flashlight on the black lacquer dressing table, careful to avoid the mirror behind it. This was supposed to be Colonel Smidely's room, and yet enough cosmetics to stock the stalls at Harrod's gleamed in the beam of the light. Was this part of someone's plot to catch him? And where were the diamond cufflinks he was supposed to steal? They weren't in the correct place.

He picked up a tube of lipstick and set it down in exasperation, then turned to examine the bed.

He noted a salmon coverlet, as he had seen in the other staterooms; a copy of the ship's daily activities newsletter; and an expensive eel-skin purse.

He hesitated. He wasn't supposed to go through purses.

But these were unusual circumstances, calling for some initiative. The Committee had encouraged him to improvise—within the approved guidelines, of course.

Swallowing, he snapped open the purse, wincing at the loud *clock!* as the catch released. He rummaged inside, then found the equally luxurious wallet and flicked it open to the credit-card section.

"Good. Identification," he murmured, aiming the light.

A stunning brunette wearing too much makeup smiled coyly from the lower left corner of a California driver's license. Sucking in his breath, he nearly dropped the wallet. Somehow he'd stumbled into none other than the seductive Mara Northcoate's stateroom. Talk about the most dangerous spot on the ship . . .

No, there was one other, far more dangerous. He thought of the lovely Amy and shook his head. That kiss had changed his life. He was mad for her. And she had gone on about Errol Flynn!

He smiled, remembering her huge eyes, how feather-light she had been in his arms as they had waltzed around the dance floor. Her hair was golden and her skin was Devon cream. Oh, she was exquisite, she who taught torches to burn bright.

"And you're going to stand still long enough for me to convince you of it, Amy van Teiler," he murmured as he snapped off the flashlight.

Peeling off his gloves, he stuffed them and the flashlight into the pockets of his tuxedo jacket and hunkered by the porthole. With his forefinger, he drew back the curtain and peered out for almost a full minute before satisfying himself that the coast was clear. Then he opened the door as quietly as he could and stepped into the bracing night air.

Not a soul stirred outside. Derek grinned, immensely pleased with himself. Either he was very lucky or else he had an excellent sense of timing. Three break-ins since the start of the voyage and not a single witness.

He was feeling so invincible that he didn't even bother to keep to the shadows as he strode away. He even began to whistle.

Which was why, Amy decided as she watched Derek disappear around a corner, he didn't hear her surprised cry when he thrust open Mara's door, nearly smashing it into her face as she stood behind it. And why he didn't hear her softly moan, "Oh, darn," as he walked off in the opposite direction without realizing she'd been inches away from him.

Swallowing, she clutched her shawl around her shoulders and walked back to her cabin.

Sitting on her bed with her shoulders slumped, she toyed with the fringes of her shawl. What had she expected? What, really? As Mrs. Bordon put it, he was an "adventurous" man. And Mara was an adventurous woman.

Amy drummed against the mattress with her fingers. "Just because he made a pass at you . . ." She trailed off, remembering her lush, romantic dream, and grimaced. "Time to grow up, Amy. You're no one's fairy princess."

But oh, it would be so nice to be . . .

"No," she told herself firmly. "That's not real life. Now, go to sleep."

After a long struggle, she did sleep. And dreamed more dreams of Derek Morgan, as she was sure millions of other women did too.

*   *   *

To Amy's chagrin, Mara appeared at breakfast looking thoroughly pleased with the world. She was gracious to everyone, even insisting that Amy try some of her scrambled eggs à la Marguerite. For Giovanni she had a special smile, one that ended with a fluttering of the lashes à la Scarlett O'Hara. While she nibbled daintily on the eggs, Giovanni devoured her with his eyes and she turned this way and that, as if to give him more to gobble up.

Amy found it incredible that Mara could flirt with their waiter so intensely after spending a night of passion with Derek. She was as good an actor as he was.

Ten minutes later Derek paraded into the dining room, surrounded by a bevy of beautiful young women. They were all laughing and chatting animatedly, touching his hands, his arms, his cheeks.

Not that Amy blamed them: he looked magnificent, in an outsized white linen jacket and matching trousers and a peach-colored shirt. The pastel tones set off his rich tan and black hair and the unearthly obsidian cast of his eyes. He was even more handsome this morning than he had been last night, if that were possible.

He looked in her direction. Amy shifted her attention to something Mrs. Bordon was saying and sipped her coffee with feigned nonchalance. He was staring at her; she could feel it, as if he were boring a hole through her with a white-hot laser. Shifting beneath the heat of it, she wondered why he wasn't staring at Mara this morning. After all, she was the one who had made him whistle.

Amy had resolved to ignore him, and she did her level best. But her eyes kept straying to his table, just for a little peek at him, and each time she looked, he stopped whatever he was doing and gazed at her.

Then, when he rose from his table and started walking toward hers, she excused herself quickly and left the dining room.

She didn't see him again all day, and was appalled at her own disappointment. And later that night, when she spied him sneaking into yet another stateroom, her spirits plunged even further.

"So. Better safe than sorry," she muttered under her breath as he let himself into the darkened room.

And she *was* sorry, though she still didn't feel safe. No, not safe at all.

The next morning, the fourth day of the cruise, Derek breezed into the dining room alone. Sensing danger, Amy rose in an attempt to breeze out, making it to the wall of glass before he sidestepped her and caught her hand.

"Good morning, Lady Sunshine," he said cheerily, raising her knuckles to his lips.

"Good morning," she replied, straining to sound cool and unimpressed by his gallantry. But how could she, when the brush of his mouth against her skin sent electricity zinging through her bloodstream?

And how could she, when he looked so perfect, in a white cotton bib shirt and royal-blue cotton slacks? Beside his contemporary elegance, she felt silly in her thirties-style middie blouse and matching red skirt, but she forced down the feeling and shifted her weight on rubbery legs.

"How have you been?" he asked, and before she could answer, he said, "Come sit with me. I haven't had breakfast yet."

"We all have seating assignments," she said

through clenched teeth. "And I've already had my breakfast."

"Please?" He dipped his head and peered at her through his lashes like a little boy pleading with his mother for the puppy that had followed him home.

"I would think you'd rather have breakfast with . . . someone else." She jerked her hand away. Instantly there was a buzz of discussion around them: *What was happening between Derek Morgan and the woman he'd left with two nights ago?*

He chuckled. "Who on earth would that be?"

Ignoring his lightheartedness, she dug into her purse and held up the black lace fan. "The owner of this, maybe," she challenged, "or how about Mar—"

He went white. "Oh, my Lord, put that away!" he whispered, closing his hand around the fan. He lowered it to her side and hid it in the folds of her skirt.

"What on earth . . . ?"

"Ssh. Please. Just help me get to the table so we can put it back into your purse." His heavy brows furrowed over his deep-set eyes. "Please, Amy. I beg of you. Or I'm doomed."

"What? What are you talking about?"

He took a breath and tightened his grip on the fan nestled in her skirt. His fingers brushed her thigh and her leg muscles tensed. "Please."

"Well . . . okay."

He sighed heavily, shutting his eyes for a flicker of an instant. "Thank you."

Then he placed her hand over the fan, pressing it against her leg, and threaded his arm through hers. He led her toward the captain's table, all pleasant smiles and greetings now as some of the other diners hailed him.

With total ease, Derek introduced Amy to the

other passengers at the table—the captain himself was absent—chatting as if he hadn't a care in the world. Then he propelled Amy into an empty chair and sat down beside her, whispering, "Where did you get that bloody fan?"

"I . . . I found it." Shielded by the ivory tablecloth, she opened her purse and smuggled the offending article into it. "You dropped it the other night."

"I . . ." His eyes widened in horror. "I did?"

"Yes, when you were coming out of that state—"

"Ssh!" Casually he looked to the left and right. "Someone might hear you."

"Oh." She frowned. "So?"

"Coffee?" he asked her as a waiter glided near. Absently she nodded. *"Due, per favore,"* he told the waiter. He turned to Amy. "I'll be ruined if anybody sees that fan."

"Oh." She paused. "How?"

"I . . ." He bit his lower lip. "I can't tell you, sweeting."

Because it belonged to a woman, she filled in mentally, and he was still trying to beguile Amy into going to his stateroom.

The waiter brought the coffee. Amy stirred in some cream, watching the swirls of white and brown so she wouldn't have to look at Derek. If she did, she was afraid he would be able to see what she was thinking.

She sighed, inhaling a sandalwood aroma she knew to be his. He always smelled delicious. And took good care of his nails, too, she noted as he dropped two sugar cubes into his cup. Was *everything* about him perfect?

"I missed you yesterday," he said suddenly. "I even had a dream about you. It was a strange dream, filled with battles and knights and ladies." He laughed. "It sounds like a bad movie."

No, she replied wordlessly. It sounded like *her*

dream from the night they'd met. Only two days ago! Mrs. Bordon was right; the shortness of the cruise accelerated one's sense of time. In five days they'd dock in Southampton.

"You're angry with me about the fan," he observed.

Quickly she shook her head. "Not at all. Why should I be?"

"Lucky thing for you you're not an actress," he said dryly. "All right, I'll confess. I . . . it's for a . . ."

"Yes?" she asked, looking at him.

He paused. Then he smiled apologetically. "Amy, I just can't tell you. I'm sorry."

"Well, it's really none of my business," she said, picking up her cup and taking a gulp.

The coffee was scalding. She gasped as she slammed down the cup and reached wildly for some water.

"Don't be upset," he said softly, covering her hand with his. "It's not what you're thinking."

"I'm not . . . upset!" she croaked, clutching her neck. "Give me some water!"

Instantly he let go of her hand and grabbed his water glass. "I'm sorry! Here, love," he urged, pressing it against her mouth.

She took it from him and drank the whole thing down without stopping for breath. Her throat burned like fire.

"Are you all right?" he asked when she set the glass down. He reached for another, but she held up her hand.

"Enough. Yes, I'm all right. But you're dangerous!" She pushed back her chair. "And devious."

He caught her wrist. "Amy, don't go."

"I'm already history," she said haughtily, though she was taken aback by the look of abject entreaty on his face.

"Lady Sunshine." His eyes became dewy, and

she found herself sitting on the edge of her seat, unmoving, falling into his gaze. "I need the fan."

Her heart sank. And she'd had the audacity to imagine, for the shortest of moments, that the third word in that sentence might have been "you." She was still living in dreamland. She opened her purse.

"No, not here. Not in public," he said.

She snapped the purse shut. "Why not? Is she married?"

"Amy, I don't even know her," he insisted. "I'm not sure I could pick her out in a crowd. With her regular clothes on, I mean."

"You know, you're rather crude," Amy remarked tartly, and rose. "But maybe some women find that attractive."

"Amy . . ." He reached for her.

Head held high, she opened her purse. When he began to rise, she pointed her finger at him and said, "Stay," thinking of that puppy-dog look of his that only moments ago had mesmerized her. "Or I'll expose you to the world." Meeting his gaze, she slid her hand threateningly into her purse.

Suddenly he laughed, a low, rolling guffaw that emanated from his chest and sent ripples up her spine. "All right. Have it your way. You've won the battle." He grinned devilishly at her and picked up his coffee. "But you haven't won the war."

"Humph." She smiled at the other occupants of the table. "It was nice to meet you," she told them, and they smiled back and bobbed their heads.

Then she looked at Derek. "I'll give the fan to the purser," she whispered. "You can get it from him."

"No! He might be in on it. In the book . . ." Derek made a fist and pounded it softly against his lips as if to reproach himself for saying too much. "Bring it to my stateroom." When she raised a single, wispy brow in response, he shrugged and said,

"Then just put it in a box and give it to me at lunch."

She eyed him. "But I might not see you at lunch."

"Yes, you will." It was almost as if he were ordering her to appear—Taras Bulba issuing commands to one of his minions. His forceful attitude both irritated and fascinated her.

"I might not even have lunch."

"Yes, you will."

She bristled. "Well, you're certainly sure of yourself, aren't you?"

To her surprise, Derek shook his head and whispered, "No, love. I'm just good at acting as if I am."

"Come, two more for Egg and Spoon!" Mrs. Bordon trilled.

It was later in the day—Amy had resolutely skipped lunch—and now she was sitting in a wooden steamer chair along the green, orange, and blue mosaic wall of the ship's indoor pool. Around her, tiled cupolas and balconies swirled with the reflected water of the "Pompeian Bath," as the pool was called.

Swathed in her silver-gray velour robe, Mrs. Bordon stood in front of Amy and clapped her hands. "Come, Amy, dear. Play my silly game."

"All right," Amy said obediently. She would do anything Mrs. Bordon asked, though her heart wasn't in silly games at the moment. She would have preferred to sit in her steamer chair and think about the startling idea that had been forming in her mind since breakfast.

What if Derek were crazy?

Oh, not *very* crazy, not lock-'em-up crazy, but what about the way he had gone on about the fan, and muttering that the purser might be in on it? In on what? The *purser*?

"Listen to the rules, dear!" Mrs. Bordon chided Amy.

Amy bobbed in the eleventh lane of the pool in a copy of Claudette Colbert's swimsuit for *Bluebeard's Eighth Wife*, stitched in cool green with gold bamboo designs to highlight her hair. The ten other swimmers were similarly dressed in thirties suits, all gazing fondly at Mrs. Bordon as she placed a spoon in her mouth and balanced an egg in the bowl.

"Mmpf?" she queried. She pulled out the spoon. "And then you swim with the spoon in your mouth for three laps. That's all, darlings!"

"Why three, Aunt Geneva?" Mara asked in a bored voice as she tugged at the modest cut of her crimson suit. She was watching from the sidelines, her expression hovering between ennui and mortification over her great-aunt's antics.

"Because that's what I just made up!" Mrs. Bordon laughed. "That's the way it was then. We invented the most outrageous games on the spot. We never really planned anything except the costume balls." Her eyes twinkled. "It was spontaneous." She smiled at Amy. "Like romance."

Amy flushed at Mara's knowing chuckle and turned an even deeper shade of crimson when Mrs. Bordon bent down from the side of the pool, held out a spoon and egg, and nodded approval as Amy slid the spoon between her teeth.

"Very good, dear. And your suit looks so cute." She patted Amy on top of the head and moved to the next contestant.

Cute? On Colbert it had been nothing short of dangerous—rather like Mara's looked on her. No wonder Derek had come out of her stateroom whistling. Mara had a lot to whistle at.

Dum-dum, you said no to him! she reminded herself, but still she felt unreasoning anger as she assumed the start-off position and tensed for the sound of the Chinese gong, which a steward held out for Mrs. Bordon.

Unreasoning anger, her foot, Amy admitted to herself. She was plain jealous.

Of a hussy and a crazy man? *Her?* Not bloody likely! Oh, listen, now she was even talking like him!

"Go!" Mrs. Bordon cried as the gong clanged.

She was not jealous, she was not. How utterly ridiculous! Amy's legs and arms pumped in rhythm with her silent protests; then her thoughts turned to images of Derek from *Taras Bulba:* his hairy, sinewy chest, the ripples of muscles in his abdomen, the intriguing jut of his pelvic bones. Muscles like rock, like polished stone—oh, how had he avoided crushing her when they had waltzed? How, those many times, had he not bruised her hands when he had caught them up in his large grip? Because he had tamed his body to be gentle with women—when he wanted to be gentle. . . .

"Amy! You're the winner!" Mrs. Bordon sang out.

Amy blinked, bewildered, and took the spoon from between her teeth. Now she had eaten an entire dinner and won a race in total oblivion because of him.

She climbed out of the pool and accepted her prize—a small silver commemorative medal of the *Meg*'s last crossing—and Mrs. Bordon's congratulatory kiss on the cheek.

"Thank you," Amy said, bemused, toweling herself with the heavy square of white terry cloth the steward handed her. "I owe it all to the pond on my brother-in-law's ranch."

Where many a midnight she had slipped into the silky water completely nude, and danced with the stars and dreamed of heroes . . .

"Surely you're not leaving now?" Mrs. Bordon asked plaintively as Amy stepped into her sandals and pulled a lavender gauze caftan over her head. "Oh, but that's quite all right if you want to, dear. You're free to do as you wish," she added quickly.

"Maybe she has a rendezvous," Mara drawled, barely hiding her smirk.

Amy flared inside, but kept her face impassive. "I wanted to work on a few things of Mara's," she told Mrs. Bordon. "Some of her seams need to be let out."

"How kind of you." Mrs. Bordon smiled so guilelessly that Amy regretted her cattiness. "Be sure to keep track of how many hours you work, dear. I'm going to pay you. And don't forget the séance tonight. It will be such fun."

Amy wrapped the towel into a turban around her hair. "I'm sure it will, Mrs. B. Thanks again for the prize."

She left the Pompeian Bath and took the corridor designated for swimmers. The floor was made of hard rubber, made slippery and slick by small pools of water caused by dripping bathing trunks and bikinis. " 'Maybe she has a rendezvous,' " she echoed, mimicking Mara's suggestive tone. "She's so *sure* of herself!"

Adjusting her turban, she remembered how she'd said that to Derek at breakfast. *I just act as if I am, love.* Was that true? When was Derek acting and when was he being sincere?

"Oh! Excuse me!" Amy cried out as she collided with an elderly gentleman tottering around the corner. Her arms flailed, but she couldn't seem to catch him as he sank to the floor, his cane falling, *swok!* into a puddle of water. She'd been too engrossed in her own thoughts to notice him, and she'd ploughed right into him.

The man lay sprawled in a heap of arms and legs, a lined, pasty-gray face wreathed with a beard, smiling cheerily up at her. Behind gray-tinted glasses, his dark eyes twinkled. He wagged his finger at her, his hand shaking badly. "*Ach, nicht* problem, *fraulein*. As you can see, I am all right."

"Let me help you up," she insisted, moving to take his hand, but he shook his head and pointed to a leather-bound book beside her left foot. "Better to save that, *ja*? It is not so old as me, but likes water less."

"Oh, I'm sorry! I hope it's not ruined!"

Amy scooped it up at once as the man planted his feet beneath himself and crawled up his walking stick to bring himself to a standing position.

"You see? I am fine," he announced.

"Well, I'm very sorry," Amy said. She glanced down at the front of the book. *"Mayhem on the Margaret."* She smiled at the old man. "Is this about the *Meg*?"

"Ach, ja," he replied. Stooped with age, he wore a baggy tweed jacket and wool trousers, which gave him a professorial air. *"Ein* mystery story."

Her eyes widened with interest. "Really! Where did you find it?"

In reply, he chuckled and tapped his head. When Amy gave him a puzzled smile, he explained, "I wrote it. In German first, then it is translated by my nephew." He leaned toward her conspiratorially. "You must know about the big mystery group on board, *ja*? This is *mein* book they are using."

"I'm sorry, but I don't understand," Amy said.

He thought for a moment. "They are on this ship as a group. Every two years they do this. For this voyage, they planned everything back in America, then gathered together. You know, for a special kind of party cruise for mystery peoples."

As Mrs. Bordon's was a special party. "That sounds like fun."

"You don't know about it? I thought maybe you are playing, with such old-style robe and shoes. And headdress—you are Scheherazade, *ja*?"

Amy chuckled. "No, I'm not playing. But I'd love

for you to tell me about it. This group got together to read your book, you say?"

"*Nein, nein.* They take ideas from the book. Someone makes a script and gives out parts for each one to play. They must solve *ein* big mystery. In *mein* story, it is a series of jewel robberies. In America, I believe you call them 'heists.' "

"Really? But how does it work?"

He held up a finger. "First, they know each other only in costumes. You see, most of the book happens at *ein fantastiches* costume ball on *der* ship. So, these mystery people dress up, you see? But they do not recognize each other when they are in normal clothes. They may eat at the same breakfast table, and never guess! There are thirty of them, and they all have cabins in first class."

He smiled and held up a second finger. "But only the thief knows which cabins belong to mystery *gruppen.*"

Amy clapped her hands together. "There's a thief? How intriguing!"

"Of course. He steals jewelries the others must leave out for him to take. The game is to catch him." He made a fist. "To unmask him. It could be any one of them."

Somewhere deep in Amy's brain, the beginnings of some connections formed. A mystery group, using a book? Hadn't Derek mentioned something's being "in the book"? That the purser could be "in on it"?

"He breaks into their cabins and takes things?" she asked in a dramatic undervoice.

The old man leaned toward her. "Only permitted jewelries, *ja*, he does. They are, what do you say, proops?"

"Props?" Her eyes widened.

"*Ja, danke.* The other people must discover who he is. Then the game is *fertig.* Over."

The connections became stronger. "By any

chance, is there a fan involved? A Spanish fan?"
she asked excitedly.

For a moment she thought the old gentleman
was going to laugh. Instead he nodded. "Bravo,
fraulein! Good guess. *Ja.* Part of the game is that
the thief leaves it in a room. Accidental. For *ein*
clue to his iden . . ."

"Identity?"

"Precisely."

Amy bit her lower lip to keep from giggling.
Derek! The fan! The purser! The staterooms! She
saw it all. He was playing the part of the thief!

Well, she didn't see *exactly* all. Mara wasn't in
the mystery tour. Her room hadn't been the setting
for *that* kind of "scene of the crime."

"But all someone has to do to catch the thief is
read your book." She riffled through the pages,
then flipped to the end.

"Nein," the old man said gently, taking the book
from her. "You see, *fraulein,* this mystery group
has taken certain . . . what do you say, liberties
. . . with the book to make their party. I am only
the basis. Big honor for old man from Wiesbaden,
nicht so?" He puffed out his chest, which once
must have been muscular but now seemed thin
and bony.

"Oh, yes," Amy said, eyeing the book. She smiled
weakly. "At least he's not crazy."

The man cupped his ear. "Please?"

"Nothing. I said nothing worth repeating."

The man nodded. "I see. I am Otto von Herzschmerz, at your service." He offered his hand.

Amy took it. His grip was strong and firm, his
flesh smooth and warm. There was something
about his handshake that reminded Amy of someone else, but she couldn't quite place it. "Amy van
Teiler."

"Ah, Dutch name," he said warmly. "I have relations in *Nederlands*. Well, good-bye. Perhaps we see us on the ship."

"Oh, I hope so!" Amy replied.

Suddenly von Herzschmerz held out the book. "Here. You take it. I have other copies." When she demurred, he thrust it into her hands. "Happy reading," he said, and hobbled past her toward the pool.

"Thank you, Mr. von . . ." She looked down at the cover of the book to check his name. "Mueller?" But that didn't sound at all like what he'd told her.

The old man stopped. "Von Herzschmerz," he called. "Name on the book is not *mein* real name."

"Well, thank you," she said. "I really appreciate it."

He turned and smiled at her. "I hope you enjoy *mein* little story."

"I'm sure I will." She smiled back as he minced down the corridor.

Amy spent the rest of the day in her cabin reading *Mayhem on the Margaret*. When she was finished, she was absolutely, positively sure that Derek was playing the role of the thief.

It made sense: the way he'd been dressed the first time she'd seen him, all in black, with gloves, and with that sack slung over his shoulder; the fan and his horror at being caught with it in public. His secrecy.

She made a face. What about his lust for Mara?

Well, almost all of it made sense. And in a different context, lusting after a woman like Mara made perfect sense, too—if you were a superficial, loutish, Errol-Flynn kind of man.

"Oh, but he's not," she told her reflection in the dressing-room mirror. "He can't be, not deep down."

Her mirror image gazed back at her. Why not? it seemed to demand. Because then he couldn't be your Prince Charming? The big hero? Remember, Amy, dear, this is the real world, where people have flaws, and things don't always turn out the way you wish they would. He probably really is a superficial, loutish, Errol-Flynn type of man.

Amy closed the book. "I hate reality," she mumbled, and closed her eyes.

And dreamed . . . of a masked man dressed in a black cape, riding a jet-black horse through the forest. Gal-lop, gal-lop, the steed's hooves thundered, shooting tremors through the earth.

He was a broad-shouldered man, tall in the saddle, hunching to avoid overhanging branches. His angular jaw was set in a grim line; a muscle jumped in his cheek as his horse sailed over a fallen log. His eyes burned like coals ringed with wooded shadow as they darted over the landscape, searching.

And then he found her, the golden-haired glory of his life, gesturing in the doorway of the old inn to go back, go back, it was a trap!

Bullets flew from the rifles of the hidden soldiers. But still the man urged the horse forward. He lurched as he was hit; blood streamed down the arm of his fine linen shirt and dripped on the tooled Spanish saddle, but he paid his wound no heed.

She ran to him; he leaned out of the saddle and swept her up behind him, and they flew like the wind, his cape shielding her from the bullets as he rescued her from that fearsome place. . . .

Amy woke up and groaned as she realized she had dreamed of Derek again.

"This is getting to be a bad habit," she muttered.

The Elizabethans believed your lover obsessed you, that you could think of nothing else. The cruel curse of love made kings foolish and toppled realms. It sent young lovers to their doom. It upset the very forces of nature.

It was to be avoided at all costs.

"Fine with me," she muttered. "Absolutely no problem."

Four

Later that night, Derek smiled as the well-costumed members of Geneva Bordon's party introduced themselves to the equally well-costumed participants of the International Society of Mystery Fans. To hide their identities, the ISMF members always dressed in costume when they convened, and now Charlie Chan, Agatha Christie, a Spanish lady of mystery, and a sultan—among others—mingled with men and women dressed in the finest fashions of the thirties. Everyone had assembled in the main lounge, once the gentleman's smoking room in more gracious, although perhaps more chauvinistic, days, and now the setting for Mrs. Bordon's séance.

"Good evening. I'm Geneva Bordon," the dear old lady said to Derek, holding out her hand. "And you must be Zorro."

Drat, why hadn't he thought of Zorro? Derek mused, shaking her hand. He'd worried that his highwayman's outfit proclaimed his role a bit too obviously, but banked that the ISMF'ers—a sophisticated lot—would imagine the costume to be something of a red herring, worn to distract attention from the real thief.

"Nay, milady, 'tis a simple roadside robber I be," he replied in a rough voice.

"A highwayman!" she trilled. "How very exciting! I'm so glad I invited your group to my little soiree."

"As be we, milady. 'Twas a right generous gesture on your part."

"Perhaps we shall conjure up the spirit of a *real* highwayman," she suggested.

"Mayhap."

"Let me introduce you to some of my people," she went on. "Oh, look, there's Amy," she cried, gesturing.

Derek turned.

Amy was staring at him as though she'd seen a ghost. Her face was the color of the simple ivory satin gown she wore, as she stood with her hands clenched together. Dainty bell sleeves accentuated the curve of her arms and her fragile, petite quality, the vulnerability that triggered a strong protective reaction in him.

"That's Amy van Teiler," Mrs. Bordon said. "She's a young friend of mine who designed all our costumes and . . ."

He didn't hear any more. His entire attention was focused on Amy. She looked shocked by his appearance, nearly paralyzed with surprise.

He knew she recognized him, and he thought he understood her alarm. Did she really think he'd give up on her so easily? Look at how she stood, rooted to the spot. He swallowed. For her, he wanted to be a knight in shining armor, and he found himself wishing he were better, stronger, richer, cleverer, just so he could be whatever she needed and wanted. At the very least, less intimidating. Why couldn't she be more like Mara, who had made it abundantly clear that she wanted to have an affair with him?

What on earth was he thinking? Mara was the *last* person in the world he wanted Amy to be like.

To compare her to that woman was . . . blasphemous. Amy was an angel, sweet and almost supernatural in her beauty. Mara was nothing if not earthy.

"Excuse me," he said to Mrs. Bordon, and strode across the room to Amy's side. Her eyes grew wider, like great, glittering topazes, framed by her shiny golden hair. He saw her take a breath, steadying herself for his approach—but not running, he noted thankfully. Not escaping him.

Just as he reached her, music spilled into the room—a scratchy gramophone playing a seductive tango—and without a word he swept her into his arms.

Her eyes were huge; her lips parted silently as he gathered her up and moved her in the sultry dance. She smelled like roses, her skin petal-soft and rose-white. He longed to kiss her temple, her cheeks, her pliant, soft mouth and beg her to lose herself in a fantasy with him.

Let's pretend we're in love, he wanted to tell her. *Let's pretend this moment will last forever and ever.*

His cape furled around them, shielding her from the others as they dipped. His hands cradled her back and waist as he draped her backward, bending over her. Her neck arched as she stared up at him, and he had to fight not to run his mouth along the slender column and bury his face in her breasts.

He was not new to sexual attraction—as the latest overnight sensation, he had women all over the globe throwing themselves at him—but the force of the erotic power that emanated from Amy enthralled him. Here was a mature woman who trembled like a schoolroom dove; here were passion and fire beneath modest delicacy; here was the deep throbbing of ancient rhythms beneath the shallow rise and fall of her breasts as she stared wordlessly at him.

Say you love me, he found himself asking her silently, not able to take his eyes off her. *Say you love me, even if you don't and never will.*

Then the music ended. Amy gave a little cry and worked her way out of his arms.

"Stop this," she said. "Stop . . . *badgering* me."

He held out a hand. "Amy, dear love—"

She shook her head. "I'm not interested, Derek."

"Shh," he said, flinching. "No one's supposed to know who I am." When she looked disbelieving, he shrugged, and added, "Geneva didn't. Neither did Mara."

"*That's* hard to swallow."

He gave her a crooked smile and tried to hold her hand. In response, she crossed her arms, wrapping her fingers around her elbows. She was trembling.

"Derek, please don't. You know I find you . . . I think you're . . . I'm . . ." She raised her liquid, dark-honey eyes to his, and he melted. He understood that she found him threatening, but how the devil could he get around that? How did one woo a woman who spent most of her time running in the other direction as if you were Count Dracula himself?

"Time for the Ouija boards!" Mrs. Bordon sang out. "Everybody make groups of four, and the stewards will pass them out."

Derek forced a wan chuckle. "She's kidding, isn't she?"

"You two must be partners!" Mrs. Bordon declared, thrusting a Ouija board into Derek's arms and a small, triangular-shaped piece of plastic into Amy's hands. "Get two more and find a table!" She sailed on.

Amy swallowed. "I'd rather not."

Derek shifted the board under his arm and put a hand on her shoulder. She jumped.

In a flash of an instant he knew what he must do. Summoning all his acting skill, he forced down his true feelings and replaced them with a casual but polite smile and loosened the tenseness in his jaw and spine. He patted her easily and said, "Look. I think I know how you feel about me"—secretly he exulted as she blushed—"and I want to start over. I've come on too strong with you, and I apologize. How about this? We'll be friends. Keep things light and fun. No more chasing you around the ship like a sex maniac."

Her shoulders actually drooped. Derek's heart leaped with the realization that she was crushed. She feared him, but as he had suspected, she also wanted him. His intuition had proved correct—the hard sell wouldn't work with her. Recalling his older sister's tactic of playing hard-to-get with the village boys who used to come around their home, he saw the wisdom in the ploy. It relieved the pressure and allowed the chemistry to work. It piqued the interest.

"I mean it," he promised, mentally congratulating himself on his fine performance. "Truly, Amy. I'll keep my hands to myself."

She looked uneasy. "But you—"

"Please," he said winningly.

For a moment he was afraid she was going to launch into a speech about men like Errol Flynn, but instead she cocked her head as she considered, then finally nodded.

"That would be . . . nice," she said resolutely, as if convincing herself. Her smile was a beguiling combination of uncertainty, shyness, and honesty. "After all, I've never been friends with a world-famous movie star before."

"Nor I with an escapee from the thirties," he replied. Why she believed him he had no idea; up until then, she had never accepted him at face value. He must sound sincere.

He gestured at her dress. "Remember those old 'Mummy' movies? I used to love watching them on the telly late at night. In that white dress you'd be perfect as the damsel in distress."

He hunched over and rolled his hands over each other. "And I shall be the man in the fez, burning tana leaves in the Masonic temple in Lost Angeles," he went on in a perfect Boris Karloff imitation. "Preparing to whisk you off to the late, late show."

She blessed him with the laugh that made the nerves along his spine dance, and he mentally shook his head in wonderment that in exchange for a few words of assurance she was giving him so much warmth and friendliness.

"Did you call it that on purpose?" she asked delightedly. " 'Lost' Angeles?"

"Certainly, my dear. I know of no other place on earth as lost as that. So we're friends," he stated, returning to the subject. "Let's shake on it."

This time she let him take her hand. Energy surged through him, making his fingers jerk and his heart thunder. It was as if a bond were growing between them, a physical joining, and he thought of his glib remark at the dinner table about soul mates. Could such a phenomenon exist?

"Everyone take a table! Find partners!" Mrs. Bordon commanded, clapping her hands. "The unknown awaits us!"

Indeed, Derek thought. The unknown did await them.

They found two partners—Geronimo Jones and Mildred Hopkins, neither of whom seemed to recognize the highwayman as Derek, and then they all sat down to a small table draped in black and silver. Derek unfolded the Ouija board and spread it over the table. Amy set the triangle of plastic in the middle of the board, directly parallel with the inscribed words *Yes* and *No*. Across the top ran the alphabet, and in the center of the board there were numbers. *Good-bye* was written below them.

The stewards poured glasses of brandy before they retired, and now all set themselves to the busy task of raising ghosts.

"Put your fingers on top of the planchette," Amy explained to Geronimo, who was confused about what to do. Her own fingers brushed Derek's, and below the table their knees touched. Derek thought he was going to shoot through the ceiling.

"Let's go," he said in his gruff, highwayman's voice. "I'll ask the first question. Is anyone here?"

The planchette began to move. "YES."

"Who?"

"T-H-I-E-F," Mildred Hopkins spelled out as the planchette pointed to the individual letters. "There's a thief!"

Derek's lips parted, and he stole a glance at Amy. The corners of her mouth were twitching and her eyes were glittering. She was the one moving the planchette. Oh, the minx, the little minx, she thought she was so clever.

"What kind of thief?" Mildred Hopkins asked excitedly.

Derek watched Amy's smug look change to consternation when he discreetly took control of the planchette. The others watched the little piece of plastic zoom over the letters of the alphabet.

Mildred Hopkins frowned. "Jewelries? Is that a word?"

"J-A," the planchette spelled.

Across the table, Amy's mouth dropped open, and she looked questioningly at Derek.

For an answer, he winked. Yes, he was Otto von Herzschmerz, he silently told her, enjoying her astonishment. But he hoped he hadn't foretold his own future when he'd whimsically—and in very ungrammatical German—named himself "von Heartbreak."

Suddenly the room went black. Above the startled murmurs rose a cry.

"Help! Someone's stolen my diamond bracelet!" Mrs. Bordon shouted.

After a split second of alarm, Derek's first impulse was to fly from his chair in an effort to seize the culprit—good Lord, a *real* thief!—but small fingers shyly sought his; tremulous fingertips touched the ends of his nails. Ah, the vixen, he thought happily, closing his hand over the shaking one. He felt masculine and protective as they sat in the dark, holding hands.

Then Amy's lips were at his ear, saying, "How did you do it?"

Before he could answer, the lights came back on.

"Nobody move!" cried a voice. It was one of the stewards. "I'm going to get the captain."

"I held hands with Derek Morgan," Mildred Hopkins said dreamily, staring down at Derek's fingers entwined with hers. "I knew it was you when I looked into your eyes." But the others at the table weren't listening because Mrs. Bordon was crying and Mr. Bordon was comforting her, saying, "Shh, Geneva, dear. It will be all right."

"But someone took it!" Mrs. Bordon wailed. "Someone right here in this room."

"Our Ouija board said there was a thief," Geronimo volunteered. The room buzzed.

"Derek, you should tell them," Amy whispered, frowning at him. "Look how upset Mrs. Bordon is."

"Amy, how could I steal it? I was here all the time. I'm not Houdini," he murmured under his breath. "Honestly."

Amy bit her lip. "You didn't do it? You mean someone else did?"

"I imagine so."

"Why, here it is, Aunt Geneva," Mara announced.

"Under our table! It must have slipped off your wrist."

Mrs. Bordon looked confused. "But I felt . . . at least I *thought* I felt . . ." She gave an embarrassed laugh. "Oh, dear, everyone, I've made a foolish mistake." She covered her cheek as Mr. Bordon fastened the glittering bracelet on her thin wrist. "Come, let's play charades."

Derek winked at Amy and said, "No charades for me. I must leave. I've got a date."

"Oh." She was obviously dashed. He regretted his choice of words and moved quickly to make amends.

"I mean, an appointment." His face lit up with inspiration. "Why don't you come with me?"

A look passed between them. He could see her mind working as she deciphered his invitation, and then a brilliant smile opened up her face. *Oh, Lady Sunshine, lady, lady mine,* he thought, his heart filling. *Your smile is one of life's miracles.*

"You mean . . . ?" She made a vague motion. He nodded. "Is that . . . legal?"

"I don't see why not. After all, *they're* allowed to join forces against *me* if they want to."

Amy smoothed her hands on her skirt as she stood. "Well, then, what are we waiting for?" She smiled giddily at Geronimo. "If Mrs. Bordon asks, I went for a stroll with Mr. Morgan."

"Right on." Geronimo flashed them a peace sign. "Have a good one."

Derek returned the gesture. "Make love, not war."

Geronimo nodded. "Always do."

Together Derek and Amy walked from the lounge at a sedate pace; but the moment they shut the door, they turned to each other and Amy giggled.

"I'm going to be your accomplice!" She chortled. "Oh, this is going to be such fun!"

He reveled in her childlike excitement. She was a

breath of springtime after all the worldly women he squired who were perfectly dressed, exquisitely coiffed, conversant on the correct subjects—and dull as death. He'd had more fun playing whist back in Wales with his granny than with them.

Then why did he choose such women from among the throng eager to be seen with him? Why hadn't he found himself someone like Amy before now?

Because he had wanted to prove himself, he admitted. Here he was, a poor Welsh lad, drinking champagne with London debs on private yachts; drifting from party to party on the Riviera with the daughters of billionaires; making love to world-famous actresses, cozying up to the estranged wife of a foreign diplomat—it had been heady stuff, and ego-boosting, too. These women belonged to the highest stratum of society, and they were delighted to admit him to their rarefied set. It was as he had dreamed back in the village, listening to his father's wheezing coughs, fiercely wishing that he would one day lift the family out of there, just like a magician! There would be money and big houses, fast cars and women . . . and so there were.

And one woman in particular, his single biggest mistake . . . He shook the memory away and returned to pleasanter thoughts.

He had not sought someone like Amy because he hadn't realized the superficiality of his lifestyle before he'd met her. He hadn't understood how bored he had become, how jaded his appetites were. He thought of warm evenings in the English countryside at the estate of a young widow or a rich heiress, legs and arms tangled in the satin sheets of some huge ancestral four-poster, hearts nowhere near each other's. And then he thought of Amy, the golden sunshine of the universe. She had knocked him between the eyes with her transparent honesty and her youthful *joie de vivre.* Around her, Derek, too, was excited by life.

But most of all, he had never found a woman like Amy before because, simply, there was only one Amy. And only one man could possess her—as much as any man could—and he had the sense to know he wanted to be that man.

And he knew he would have her. He had dreamed of it so hard, imagined it so vividly, that it *had* to come true. That was how he had become famous, and that was the secret of his acting. His power to shape his life lay in his imagination. He would will Amy to be his simply by wanting her, needing her, insisting upon her.

"Derek? Have you changed your mind about my helping you?" Amy asked uneasily.

He shook himself. "Of course not. I was just lost in thought for a moment."

"You looked worried," she insisted.

He flashed her a huge, bright smile. "Who, me? I never worry about anything."

And a voice inside his head taunted, You'd better. You've got five days to make her fall in love with you. Five days. So start worrying.

Ten minutes later, Amy had dressed quickly in a dark plaid shirt, black trousers, and sneakers, and gathered her hair beneath a black knitted beret. When she met Derek outside her door, he chuckled, and said, "You look like you belong to the French Resistance. A miniature Ingrid Bergman."

"Dat's me, big boy," she replied in a hideous Swedish accent. "And you look like you did the first time I saw you sneaking around."

He ran a nervous finger around the edge of his turtleneck sweater. "You know, if you've seen me break into three staterooms, how many other people have? Have I already been found out? It was my understanding that the minute someone knew who the thief was, they were to blow the whistle."

"Maybe they're having too much fun," Amy replied. She laughed. "I know *I* am!"

He gave her a friendly hug, and she impetuously hugged him back. Once he'd backed down from playing the great lover, he was a warm, interesting person, she thought. She was so glad he'd offered to be friends.

If a little wistful . . .

She remembered how, after she had gone to see *Taras Bulba* with some of her friends, all they had talked about was what it would be like to sleep with Derek Morgan.

"Utterly divine," her friend Sylvia had pronounced.

Chere had drawled, "He's probably gay," and the rest of them had pounced on her. No way! Not a man like that!

"Not with such big feet!" Kathy insisted. When asked what *that* had to do with anything, she'd explained, "Don't you know the old saying? Men with big feet have big you-know-whats!"

Replaying the conversation, Amy felt ashamed. They had been treating Derek like a sex object. How did he feel, knowing millions—*millions*—of women speculated about his prowess, dreamed of his body thrilling theirs?

She flushed. As she had, only last night?

"We'd better go," she told him.

He hesitated for a moment, then dropped his hands to his sides and said, "Right. Tally-ho."

They slunk along the side of the ship, Derek whistling the theme to the *Pink Panther* movies, sternly shushing Amy when she laughed. He rolled his eyes and flattened himself against the bulkhead when the foghorn blew, and a flurry of giggles burst from her lips.

He took her hand and they raced through the galleys and along the staff's berths, losing themselves in gales of nervous laughter; snaked around the base of an ancient, unused smokestack; and climbed a brass ladder.

"I wish I had an accent like yours," Amy said at one point. "It would sound more James Bond-ish."

"I'd love to play Bond," Derek replied thoughtfully. "I've certainly got the experience now."

They snuck through the ship, crouching out of sight whenever a mystery fan—Derek had a list—sauntered past. When they finally reached the outside of their target room, they froze: a silhouette was etched across the porthole.

"Oh, blast," Derek said under his breath. "I thought for sure this man would go to the midnight buffet. He owns a delicatessen in New Jersey, and he must weigh twenty stone."

"Two hundred eighty pounds," Amy supplied. "I've been studying up on England," she added proudly.

"Bravo, my little colonial. We'll make a civilized person of you yet," he jibed, and she socked him lightly on the arm.

He caught her wrist and tickled her ribs, then covered her mouth when she nearly shrieked with laughter. Oh, he was a wonderful, fun-loving man! She wanted to know him forever!

Easy, easy, she warned herself. In five days they would reach England. She would go her way and he, his. She to the university and the dusty tomes on muslin and he to movie locations and more women.

"Are you cold?" Derek whispered, stirring her from her morose train of thought.

"No," she whispered back, but she was shivering inside, and suddenly she felt like crying.

Brushing her cheeks, she said, "Let's wait him out. Then I'll sneak in first."

He raised a brow. "Why you?"

"Because if he catches you, it's all over. I could

just say I was lost." Eyes wide, she fluttered her lashes at him, the picture of bewildered innocence.

"You're good at that," he said, touching her cheek. "Maybe you're not as artless as I thought."

Her cheek tingled. Ignoring the sensation, she drew herself up. "I'll have you know that I once stole a comic book from a liquor store." Flushing, she added, "On a dare," to excuse herself.

"Why, you little felon!" Derek jerked on her beret like a big brother. "I'm nonplussed."

Tucking an errant curl back inside the cap, she made a face at him, then chuckled at herself. "I snuck it back into the store, though. I was afraid my aunt would find it and give me a whipping." She sobered for a moment, recalling those awful days with her aunt. She had been genuinely terrified of her. When Claire would leave for elementary school, Amy would grab her around the knees, sobbing and begging her not to leave her alone with Norma.

Derek's eyes blazed. "The idea of anybody hitting you . . ." She felt the force of his anger, saw it in the set of his jaw and his clenched fists.

"Didn't your parents spank you?" she asked.

The door to the man's stateroom opened.

Soundlessly Amy and Derek crouched behind two deck chairs. "Good, the pigeon's flying the coop," Derek whispered. "Here's the passkey. Remember not to disturb anything but the silver box. It'll be on the corner of the dressing table nearest the door."

"Gotcha, chief. I'm outta here," Amy growled. "Keep me covered."

He caught her shoulder, his large hand a tantalizing weight.

"Wait, you need gloves, or you'll leave fingerprints."

Relieved that the night hid her flushed cheeks, she straightened her shoulders triumphantly and pulled a pair of lacy black evening gloves out of her jeans pocket. "The Madonna look is still all the rage among lady thieves," she announced, slipping them on.

"A resourceful girl." He nodded with approval.

"Okay. I'm history."

"Be careful, *mon amie*," Derek pleaded melodramatically. "The fate of the cause rests on your shoulders."

She saluted him. *"Vive la France!"*

He made a face. "Please, you're talking to a Welshman."

They chuckled together. Then Amy darted to the door, inserted the key, and opened the door.

"Aha!" she whispered to herself in the darkness, feeling for the silver box. But the corner of the dressing table was bare.

Great. Now what? She should have gotten the flashlight from Derek.

Creeping back to the door, she opened it and stuck her head out, motioning for him to come.

He moved on cat's feet; she had glanced away to check the table again, and when he put a hand on her shoulder, she jumped.

"Shh," he cautioned. "Let's have a look-see."

Shielding the beam of the flashlight with his gloved hand, he examined the table. It was completely bare.

"Bloody hell," he muttered. "It's not here. These people are cheating. You know, they've even given me bad directions. The other night I ended up in Mar—"

Both of them froze at the sound of footsteps on the wooden deck. They were moving in the direction of the stateroom.

"Oh, no!" Amy whispered noisily. "He's coming back!"

Derek looked around the room, then pointed to the right.

"There's the bathroom. We'll hide in the shower."

Amy nodded and tiptoed toward the bathroom, but the man's key was already in the lock. With a breathy curse, Derek yanked open a door and thrust her into a closet, jumping in behind her.

Derek was so tall, he had to crouch, which made his backside stick out too far to allow the door to shut. Exhaling, he hunkered sideways like a skier negotiating a turn. That didn't work either.

"Kneel," Amy whispered desperately, and Derek obeyed her.

The stateroom door shut at the exact instant that Amy pulled the closet door closed.

As he slid to his knees in the cramped space, Derek's face pressed between her breasts. Amy's back arched involuntarily and her breath caught in her throat as his nose and lips nestled in the valley of sensitive skin. The plaid shirt covering her body seemed to melt away beneath the scorching heat of his nearness. At once she was on fire, the small crowns of her nipples stiffening as her chest burned with the white heat of his breath.

His hands clasped the small of her back, and she forced herself to stand still, though she longed to undulate against him. She thought her knees would buckle but she kept them locked; thought she would sag against him, but stood straight.

Against her chest, his hair was a luxurious mink pelt, his skin sultry with the smell of sandalwood. To distract herself, she tried to listen to the sounds in the room outside, but all she could hear was Derek's shallow breathing and the wild throbbing of blood in her ears. Derek was aroused too. She could hear it in the ragged way he was breathing, and feel it in his shaking hands.

And then, when he shifted his weight, she felt the hard arousal of his manhood against her thighs, and had to force herself not to cry out. In that instant, she wanted him more sharply and fiercely than she had ever dreamed of wanting a man. It was as if her physical ability to desire had just been truly awakened; as if she had never fully experienced lust and longing before.

Beads of perspiration broke across her forehead and chest and she reeled, unaware that she was draping herself over his head. Her gloved hands raked his soft, soft hair, and she clung to him, losing herself in the ferocity of the new sensations that throbbed through her.

I must, I must, I must, her body demanded. *He must.*

It was as if her flesh had a mind of its own. She touched him everywhere she could, stretching the limits of her passion, soaring when he clung to her and she felt again his full, proud, manhood . . .

Gal-lop! Gal-lop! The promise of ecstasy thundered toward her, bearing down on her, ready to swoop her up and carry her away, away . . .

The stateroom door opened and shut. Derek thrust open the closet door with a quivering hand, and the fresh air that swept into the closet was like a light slap on Amy's face. What on earth had they been doing?

Saying nothing, not looking at her, Derek slipped away from her and stepped out of the closet.

Correction, she thought numbly. What on earth had *she* been doing? He had done nothing. Where there could have been kisses on her breasts and neck, he had not touched her. Where he could have cupped her bottom and rocked her body against his, he had not done so. Though excited, he had gallantly held himself in check. He had acted like a friend, not a lover . . . as he had promised.

"Derek, I'm sorry," she murmured, but evidently he didn't hear her. He was already across the room, peeking through the curtain.

"Derek," she said softly.

He turned around and leaned against the wall. For a moment he met her gaze, and she saw the raw longing there. Then it was gone behind an easygoing mask of wry relief. Wiping his forehead with a theatrical flourish, he gave a low whistle and said, "Boy, Ingrid, that was close."

Five

Standing next to the closet, Amy looked down at her gloves. "Yes, it was close."

Outside, the ship's horns hooted, underlining the lengthening silence between them. Where once there had been pure, unadulterated tension, now there was awkwardness, which, surprisingly, was more unsettling. Amy wondered if Derek was confused by her actions. After all her protestations and running from him, she had thrown herself at him, practically begging him to make love to her in that tiny closet! And with someone just outside the door, too. Had she gone crazy?

She peered at him. Yes, she supposed she had—and with a fierce craving for him that was like a drug. His allure was irresistible. Good-looking, charming, sexy, witty, and now friendly—he really was a fantasy man. The perfect man to share an idyllic romance on this magnificent ship, just as Mrs. Bordon had said.

Amy could just imagine what her girlfriends back home would say if they knew she was deliberately missing out on what Chere would call "the opportunity of a lifetime." To know ecstasy in the arms of Derek Morgan!

"Time we hightailed it outta heah, pardner," Derek drawled from the doorway.

"What?" Amy whipped her head up and managed a weak smile at Derek's masterful western drawl. Such a wit, too. Well, she wasn't going to waste precious time with him in mulling over what could be. She would enjoy what was . . . a friendship in the making.

"I'm a-comin'," she replied, and ambled toward him with an invisible six-shooter slung on her hip.

Derek's moonlight eyes glowed as he watched her. "Ah, you sprite," he said, and kissed her lightly on the forehead.

Then he opened the door and they both snuck out.

"Now what?" she asked. Her forehead tingled and her cheeks were hot. Maybe she had made a mistake. Maybe she should offer herself to him. The image of Mara rose in her mind. How would Amy feel if she caught him sneaking out of Mara's stateroom again? Or any of the harem of beautiful women who had accompanied him to breakfast? How would it feel to be one of the crowd, perhaps to be compared?

And found wanting?

"You look so upset," Derek said, lifting her chin between his thumb and forefinger. The moon cast shadows on his features, highlighting the planes and angles and dusting his eyes and lips with a golden sheen. "Don't worry, princess, we'll rob him in good time."

She shrugged. "And I was looking forward to it so."

"I'll make sure you won't be disappointed." He clapped his hands together. "Tell you what. Let's try another stateroom. I have lots of things to steal. Why, even a tiara. And I'll reveal where I'm stashing my booty." He slid her a glance. "Greater trust hath no thief than he that reveals his treasure location to his friend."

She bowed from the waist. "I'm honored, milord."

"I like your attitude." He dodged when she cuffed him playfully, and made threatening moves toward her rib cage. "Ready for more tickling?"

"No!" She shrieked, then clapped her hand over her mouth. "Don't make me scream," she accused him. "You'll have them all coming at a run."

He preened. "Don't I already?"

"I *thought* all movie stars were conceited."

"Just the handsome ones," he retorted, pretending to smooth his hair. "But enough about me. Let's go steal a big, juicy pair of emerald earrings."

This time the burglary went perfectly. As before, Amy unlocked the stateroom door and crept in first. A zing of exhilaration jittered up her back when her hand closed around the earrings, and she was so excited, she almost forgot to shut the door after her.

"I got them!" she whispered to Derek, who had waited by the lifeboats. She did a little dance. "I did it!"

"Bravo!" He held out his palm, and she dropped the earrings onto his glove. He grabbed them up, capturing her fingers in the process, and turned her wrist so that he could kiss the back of her hand.

"Thank you, Lady Sunshine," he said. "You've done me a great service."

Amy's airy reply caught in her throat. Oh, when he touched her, she was lost. When he looked at her . . . She steeled herself against the onslaught of tangled emotions and desires.

Ask me to go to bed again, she tried to tell him with her eyes, but he only grinned at her and tugged on the corner of her beret.

"We should celebrate. What do you want to do? Gamble? Dance? Drink?"

"Aren't we going to the stash?"

"Later, when more people are in bed."

In bed. Unbidden images of the two of them flared inside her mind. *Ask me again,* her body echoed, but he wasn't looking at her. He was staring out to sea, his profile cut from the black stone of the sky in high relief. She traced the slope of his forehead, the long, straight nose, the soft lips and hunk of jaw, memorizing each hollow and facet.

"What shall we do?" he asked, glancing up at the moon.

She thought for a moment. "Let's watch a movie."

He cocked his head and slid a glance at her. "Is that what you really want to do?"

"Why?" she asked quickly. "Don't I look like I want to watch a movie? I love movies."

There was an odd, curious light in his eyes as he replied, "Then a movie it shall be."

"Amy? Dear, are you awake?" Derek asked softly.

They were sitting in the ship's paneled library, on a well-padded sofa, facing a large-screen television and video cassette player. To their right, a fire glowed in the hearth. Derek could well imagine they were in their own home, enjoying a quiet evening. . . .

"Amy?" he repeated.

Her hand had fallen away from her popcorn and her head was resting on his shoulder. She was breathing gently, oblivious to the fact that Taras Bulba was making wild, passionate love to the captive princess on the big-screen TV. She had suggested watching it as a compliment to him, and Derek, though he found it excruciating to observe his performance on the screen, had indulged her.

"Amy, love?"

She sighed in her sleep and snuggled against him. Derek flicked off the television with the remote control and sat in the stillness, listening to Amy's gentle breathing.

If only she *were* his love. If only . . .

"Shhh, Bobo," someone whispered above him sometime later. Fuzzily Derek realized he, too, had fallen asleep. He couldn't speak; he could only listen as he drifted between the world of dreams and the world of the waking.

"Look at them, the dears," Geneva Bordon said in a gush. "Aren't they adorable?"

"Quite so, my dear."

"One wouldn't dream that man's such a wolf. Asleep he looks like an angel."

Derek felt a blanket being carefully draped over him, a hand scented with rose water tucking in the satin edge beneath his chin.

"Oh, wouldn't it be marvelous if they fell in love? She could tame him, don't you think? They say that wild men make the best husbands. I mean, look at *you*, Bobo. You were quite the gadabout when I met you. You were seeing that society girl."

"Rosa Walters." Mr. Bordon chuckled. "I do believe I heard Amy telling Mara she wasn't looking for a beau. She's too busy to think of settling down."

Derek couldn't tell if he was actually frowning or just felt like doing so. He tried to rouse himself, but he was too deeply asleep.

"I suppose you're right," Mrs. Bordon said mournfully. "And *he* certainly isn't husband material. But still, they look so perfect together. Oh, Bobo, I feel sorry for them. It never occurred to me to have a reason not to fall in love with you! All this talk of careers and all the . . . philandering they do these days. I wish they knew what we know: There's absolutely no reason good enough to postpone romance! Don't you agree, my sweet?"

"You know I do, my dear. But they hardly know each other."

"What's to know? He's a man, she's a woman. The rest will come if the foundation is there. And it only takes the blink of an eye to fall in love." She sighed. "I knew I was in love with you the moment I saw you, Bobo dear. You were playing 'Pass the Potato' at that party for the ambassador to France."

"Ah, my dear, you have such a memory. But come away now. You'll wake them."

But he *was* awake, Derek wanted to tell them. In his drowsy state he realized he was feeling a bit insulted. Not good husband material, was he?

But what did that matter? He wanted to have an affair with Amy, not marry her.

Then it came to him in a rush so strong he almost woke up: He *did* want to marry her!

"Mmmpf," he said, straining to open his eyes, but suddenly he was dreaming.

The golden-haired princess was waving to him from the burning fortress.

"Taras Bulba!" she cried. "My love, save the treasure!"

And then the sky was filled with roses, thousands of them, raining down on him. And in the center of the blossoms, she drifted inside a golden ball of light into his arms. She was nude, her lovely, small breasts dappled with the golden light, the delicate pink of her nipples caressed by the floating petals of the roses.

She helped him off with his armor and his clothes, and then she sank onto a bed of silk, her arms open to him.

"Love me, take me," she whispered. "Oh, Derek, I love you."

And then the princess was riding with him in a Rolls-Royce through the ruined landscape of the coal mines. She was wearing scarlet, with a red hat and a veil of black net with red polka dots, and she was smoking a cigarette from a long ebony holder.

"We'll steal the crown jewels and give them to your family," she told him, "and then I'll let you kiss me."

Kiss him. He felt a sigh against his mouth and opened his eyes.

Amy was kneeling over him, and when she saw he was awake, she bit her lower lip guiltily and said, "Oh, uh, hi."

He raised himself on his elbow and caught her chin. "Were you kissing me, love?"

She shook her head. "No. There was some salt on your cheek. I . . ."

His heart turned over, and he rejoiced that she was such a terrible liar. "Will you kiss me again?"

"I didn't!" Her face was bright red. When he said nothing, she blurted out, "Let's go steal something."

He smiled at her. "But you were stealing kisses. Now you have to give them back."

Her eyes grew so large, he could almost see himself in them. She wanted him. Why didn't she simply admit it?

Then he remembered what he had realized just before his dream: He wanted to marry her! To love her, and cherish her, all the days of her life.

And in a handful of days he might never see her again!

"Oh, no." Derek gasped, reeling. He felt dizzy and shaky all over, as if he had a terrible illness. That he might lose her, lose his soul mate . . .

For they *were* soul mates. He knew it now, accepted that as the reason for her overpowering effect on him, for his lightning-bolt reaction to her when they had met. They belonged together.

"Derek, are you ill? You're so white," Amy cried, putting a hand to his forehead.

So small, so cool, so silky. He wanted to fall on his knees and kiss that precious little hand, to touch his lips to the hems of her slacks. He wanted to succumb to her, melt for her . . .

"I . . ." He blinked. He couldn't believe what was going on inside him. A hurricane of every foolish, romantic image he'd ever seen or read or imagined, spun inside him like a whirling kaleidoscope. A knight in shining armor, a maiden and a unicorn; lovers parted by vendetta, by war, by tragedy, reunited through fate, magic, destiny; Romeo and Juliet, Tristan and Isolde, Abelard and Heloise . . .

Derek and Amy.

He shook his head to clear it. More images cascaded into his mind: white wedding clothes and golden rings; vows whispered in a little English country church; a moonlit bridal chamber.

"Derek?" She scrambled to her feet. "I'll get the doctor."

"No!" He grabbed her hand. Words rose in his throat. He would propose now, he thought wildly. Now, before any more time was lost.

Good Lord, get hold of yourself, he chided himself. What was he thinking of? Was he insane? They barely knew each other. And there was the very important fact that she was scared to death of him! If he proposed, she'd fly away for sure and *never* let him near her again. Then all certainly would be lost.

"No," he repeated, more calmly. "I'm sorry. I . . . I've been feeling a little seasick today. I guess it's caught up with me."

Amy pursed her lips together. "Why didn't you say so? You should be in bed. Come on. Let's call it a night."

"No."

"Derek," she said, apparently not hearing the ragged pleading in his voice, "if you're sick you should get some rest. What would happen if you couldn't finish the burglaries? It would be a mess!"

He sighed. "And I thought you might be a teensy bit concerned about me. You're only worried about losing your life of crime."

Amy turned a rosy pink. "Don't be silly. Of—of course I'm concerned about you. You're my friend, aren't you?"

He hesitated, then shrugged. "Of course I am. Of course. Bloody hell," he added below his breath.

"Derek?" she queried.

He had to sort this out. This couldn't be happening, not to him. He must be falling in love with his own fantasy of falling in love. He didn't know a thing about this woman.

"So what's to know?" Geneva Bordon's voice intruded into his thoughts. What's to know, besides the fact that somehow, in some strange, mystical way, the two of them were destined for each other?

"Derek?"

He roused himself. "I said, I'll see you in the morning," Amy told him. "I really think you need some sleep."

He reached out a hand to her, but she kept her distance, rising from the couch and putting on her beret. "Good night."

Somehow, he found his voice. "Good night."

She smiled at him shyly and left the room. As Derek watched her go, a grandfather's clock in the hall chimed two in the morning.

It was the morning of the fifth day. He had four more to go. And two days after they docked in Southampton, he was due to go on location for three months in Australia. After that he would work in Tunisia, and then Los Angeles. He might never see her again unless she went with him. And she was bound for London to accept a job. How important was it to her? How much did she want it?

In four days, could he possibly make her want him more?

Amy was in the middle of brushing her teeth the next morning when she heard someone rapping on her door.

"Blue halloo!" Derek called. "Rise and shine!"

Amy looked at herself in the mirror and groaned. She was wearing a tattered blue bathrobe, and her hair looked as if she'd taken an egg beater to it.

"The fox is afoot! The hounds await!" Derek cried cheerily. "The chase is on!"

"Argh," Amy muttered, rinsing her mouth, yet beneath her grumpiness was a wild thrill of excitement. Derek was on the other side of that door, calling for her!

She had no time to change, but she did run a brush through her hair as she walked to the door.

He must be a jogger, she thought as she glanced at the clock. It was only seven, too early for breakfast or anything else. She'd finally gotten up simply because she couldn't sleep.

"Hurry!" Derek commanded.

"I'm coming!" Amy called, unlocking the door. When she pushed it open, she burst into laughter.

She'd expected to see him in sweats, a headband holding his hair in place. But instead he was dressed in full hunt regalia, from jodhpurs and flat-heeled boots to a tweed jacket and black cap. He was flicking a riding crop against his thigh. He looked like a country squire.

"Where are the Irish setters?" she asked.

He pointed toward the stern. "My man Smythe is lunging them among the chestnuts. They're eager to go." He doffed his cap. "And so am I." He gazed at her. "You're the first woman I've ever met who looks tremendous first thing in the morning."

Amy made a face. "The trouble with actors is that they're very good at making up the worst nonsense. I know I look terrible."

"Not so! In fact, I'm just about to call the others and tell them I've found the fox." His eyes crinkled in merriment.

"Such flummery, milord." She curtsied. "But pray tell, where are you bound this morning, got up like that?"

"Why, a-hunting," he said slyly. "Or should I say, a-thieving?"

"Aren't you just a little obvious?"

He glanced down at himself with feigned astonishment. "You know, you may be right. Tell you what, you get dressed and I'll be back faster than a lord can powder his wig."

She shook her head. "You're crazy, you know that?"

"I'm an actor. All actors are crazy. My only consolation is that I get paid for it." He tapped his cap with his riding crop. "So put on your Shirley Temple duds and I'll be right back."

"As you wish, sir." Chuckling, she shut the door.

It was the kind of stunt she and Claire used to pull on each other, dressing in some outlandish costume for the sake of a silly joke. She remembered the time they had donned togas and run through the forest around the Renaissance fair encampment, flinging glitter in the air and warbling, " 'Tis spring! Forsooth!"—all just for the goony fun of it.

Ah, they had fought so hard to banish the shadows of their childhoods. Even as little girls they had played "let's pretend" with a gusto never equaled by any of their schoolmates.

"Let's pretend we're princesses," Amy would tell

her sister, and Claire would find blankets for capes and pots for crowns and big serving spoons for scepters. They would have their scepters and cry, "Off with their heads!" and "Bring Prince Charming here!" for hours.

And Norma would wallop them for making a mess.

Amy shivered as she pulled off her bathrobe. If she kept this up, she would depress herself.

Summoning up more cheerful thoughts, she put on an emerald-green wool skirt, bulky white sweater, and felt cloche hat.

"You look like a blond Betty Boop," Derek said when he returned, dressed in more conventional attire of brown corduroy slacks and a matching brown-and-white sweater.

"Boop-oop-a-doop," she said, fluttering her lashes. "Now what?"

"Now we have to spend the day working on a case, Double-O-Seven," he said in a theatrical undervoice. "Someone has moved my stash of stolen goods."

Amy's mouth dropped open. "No!"

"Yes." He stuffed his hands in his pockets as they walked into the bracing wind. "After you left last night, I went to the hold—that's where I kept it—and it was gone."

She raised her brows. "Why did you keep it there?"

He laughed. "Would you believe for security? I don't like keeping the really incriminating stuff in my stateroom, just in case someone takes it into his head to investigate me. And I can't trust the purser, either, for according to *Mayhem on the Margaret*—and the Committee, which hired me—he can be bribed."

He moved his magnificent shoulders. "I was hoping you'd help me out today. I've got to find it."

"Well, of course I will," she told him. "But what can we do?"

"I'm not sure. All this is new to me. I'm an actor, not a detective." He jingled some change in his pocket. "So now I have to act like a detective."

"You have a fun line of work," Amy observed, copying his walk. His legs were incredibly long: she had to take giant steps to keep up with him.

"It *is* fun. *Now*. It didn't used to be. I really hate starving."

"It's hard to believe you ever starved," she said. "You're a great actor."

He stopped walking. There was a wry cast to his smile as he said, "Why, thank you."

"You were super in *Taras Bulba*."

"I've done better since then," he replied cryptically.

"Oh? Have you done another movie?"

"Not yet. But I have three coming up." A storm of emotional expression crossed over his face as he spoke, but before Amy could comment on it, a sunny smile replaced it. "It's ironic to me that I now have more work than I can handle. You know what they say: When you're hot, you're hot. And let me tell you, Amy, when you're not, you most definitely are not."

He slid his hand out of his pocket and laced his long fingers between hers. She opened her mouth to protest, but he swung her arm in a jaunty way and smiled at her in an open, friendly manner. She relaxed and swung his arm, too, as the wind gusted around them and the ship plied the waters toward England.

They had breakfast together, laughing at the stir they created—*Look! He's eating breakfast with the girl from the first night!* Then they went in search of Loretta Hansen, the head of the infamous Committee that had hired Derek to be the thief.

But Loretta wasn't in her stateroom, or in the dining room, or at the pool. For hours Derek and Amy searched for her, never daring to have her paged, since that could tip off the mystery fans to the identity of the thief. Once they were besieged by a throng of Derek's admirers, who pleaded for autographs. Graciously Derek complied with their requests, then draped his arm over Amy's shoulders and murmured, "Let's hurry before more come, or we'll be stuck here for hours. And we've got to find that darn boss of mine."

"Where can she be?" Amy asked an hour later, as a steward brought a Kahlua coffee to her and hot buttered rum for Derek. It was chilly out, and much of their roaming had taken them along the ship's promenades. Derek's cheeks and nose were wind-reddened, his hair wind-tossed. He looked devilishly sexy in his sweater, deliciously appealing as he moved his shoulders as if he were still shivering.

"It's cold out," Amy said, smoothing back her hair, which she imagined must look wilder than his. The curls had frizzed in the damp salt air, and clung to her temples and forehead, then tangled along her shoulders like vines of dandelions.

"Better get used to it," Derek remarked. "That's fine English weather out there."

They were sitting in a secluded bar called the Crow's Nest, decorated in a kind of *Pirates of Penzance* theme, with hanging nets filled with barrels and shells. Two voluptuous mermaid figureheads guarded the door and Neptune himself reclined in bas relief above the bar.

"Yes, where can Miss Loretta be?" Derek echoed, sipping his drink. "Damned if I know. I'm getting a trifle irritated with the lot of them. They've even given me bad directions, you know. Why, one night I found myself in Mara's—oh, but I already told you that."

Amy leaned forward ever so slightly. "No, you didn't."

He stretched his long legs beneath the table. "I'm sure I did. The other night." He took another sip. "Maybe I got interrupted. I don't remember. Well, it wasn't important anyway."

"Oh." She traced circular patterns on the varnished tree-stump table with the moist bottom of her coffee cup. Didn't he know that anything touching on the subject of him and Mara *was* important to her? She smiled weakly. "Why don't you tell me anyway?"

He appraised her for a moment with a calculating look that made her blush—surely he was reading her mind—then set down his drink.

"I was supposed to be in Colonel Smidely's room." He chuckled. "That's what he calls himself for the purposes of the game, at any rate. But Loretta gave me the wrong stateroom numbers. I wound up in Mara's room instead." He smiled ironically. "I believe she, too, had wound up in someone else's room. Giovanni's, to be precise."

Amy lowered her head as she absorbed this revelation. Mara hadn't been in the room?

"But you came out whistling," she said before she had time to realize what she was revealing with her comment.

Across the table, Derek's lips parted. "You . . . saw me?"

Torn between confusion and happiness, she nodded.

"And you thought . . . ?"

She traced four more circles. "The obvious, naturally."

"The obvious. Naturally." Derek's tone was resigned.

Flickering light from the candle on their table cast his face in an amber glow, softening his features while it caught the gilt in his eyes. It glittered like damascene on ebony, giving him a striking, medieval air. Amy felt like singing. He hadn't slept with Mara!

"Amy, would it disappoint you horribly to know that I haven't slept with anybody since I came aboard?"

She stared at him. "Uh," she said.

"You thought I had, didn't you?"

Uneasily, she shifted. "Well, at first I did. Then I figured out you were just robbing most of them."

"Shh, sweet. You never know who might hear us. But after you read the book, what did you think? That I was still sleeping with some of those women? With Mara?"

Amy squirmed in her chair. "Well, Derek, what does it matter? I mean, you're free to do what you want. We're just friends, remember? You don't have to answer to me."

"Just . . ." He trailed off. "Yes, you're right." He flashed her a mischievous grin. "I confess—I'm trying to cultivate your high opinion of me so you'll put in a good word to Geneva. I think she's having second thoughts about adopting me."

Second thoughts. Mrs. Bordon wasn't the only one having them, Amy thought ruefully. Why *hadn't* he slept with anyone? There were plenty of lovely women on board who would give their eye-teeth for the coup of having an hour of passion with the incredible Derek Morgan. That he had been celibate didn't jive with the things Mrs. Bordon had said, or with the magazine stories Amy had read about him. Hadn't *People* called him "England's new Eros"?

She felt as if she didn't know him at all; as though a stranger had just walked up and sat down beside her.

"Tuppence for your thoughts." Derek's voice was low and soft.

"I . . . I . . ."

"Oh, damn." Derek checked his watch. "We've got to dress for the captain's cocktail party. Look. It's almost dark out."

Amy touched her earlobe and nervously toyed with a jet earring.

"I haven't been invited."

"Nonsense. You'll be my date."

That imperious tone again! Amy hid a flicker of a smile.

"Won't it be sort of . . . impolite?"

His smile was crooked and somewhat cynical. "Do you think the captain would begrudge Derek Morgan the companion of his choice?" When she shook her head, he added, "Most people have a hard time saying no to me when I ask for something."

And he hadn't asked Mara for anything! "It's not just because you're famous," she said honestly.

His eyes became hooded, his smile golden and glowing.

"I know. Let's go change."

Derek signed the tab, and then they left the Crow's Nest and walked back to Amy's stateroom. He leaned against the jamb while she opened the door, and just before she went in, he touched her hair and said, "Thank you for a marvelous day." He looked at her intently.

"You're welcome," she replied. "Why are you staring at me?"

"I was admiring your hair." He moved his head. "It looks like angel hair, all soft and shimmery around your face."

"Thank you," she said hoarsely as the door opened beneath her hand.

What if he came in? she thought. What would she do? Now that she knew him better, knew that he wasn't seeing anyone else—oh, what?

Derek, too, seemed unsure of his next action. They both stood in front of the open door with the wind gusting through their hair. Surely his heart was beating as fast as hers; his body was awakening and reaching for hers. Surely he was parting his lips to kiss her. . . .

"I'll be back for you," Derek said softly. "Will half an hour be long enough?"

His words were like a bucketful of cold water. Wilting, embarrassed, Amy nodded. "Yes, thanks."

Derek started to go, stopped, and brushed her cheek with his fingertip.

"I'll be back," he said again, and walked away.

Alone in her stateroom, Amy found a box sitting on her bed with a note attached. "Oh, dear, I've gained too much weight on the *Meg*," it read. "Could you let out the sides about an inch?" The note was signed "GB" with a flourish of curlicues and scrolls. Beneath the initials was a postscript: "And I shall pay you for the work, of course."

Amy opened the box. Inside, a copy of Mrs. Bordon's original wedding gown and veil lay nestled in a froth of blue tissue. On the last night of the voyage, the Bordons planned to renew their vows, wearing recreations of the clothes they had worn on the *Meg* in 1935. Mrs. Bordon's dress had been Amy's most important project for the cruise. She had lavished hours on it, staying up into the wee hours of many a morning to make sure it was perfect.

Amy carefully lifted the gown and veil and spread them on the bed.

A bride. A part every woman dreamed of playing at least sometime in her life. Amy fluffed the veil, admiring the gossamer quality of the yards and yards of tulle.

A bride. What would it be like, to wear a beautiful gown like this and meet a man at the foot of the church aisle, ready to pledge lifelong love to him?

Sighing, Amy smoothed the ivory satin gown. What would it be like?

Moving her shoulders in a shy little shrug, she took off her cloche hat, shoes, skirt, and sweater, then drew Mrs. Bordon's wedding dress up her legs and body, and slipped her arms carefully into the tissue-thin sleeves.

Without fastening the covered buttons in the back, she touched the rows of pearls at the bodice. There were matching pearls at the cuffs, which dropped over the backs of her hands like the sleeves of a medieval gown, and at the hem, which was too long for her.

Carefully she put on the veil. Lifting up the folds of gleaming alabaster fabric, she walked forward to let the train and the veil unfurl behind her. Then she held her hand out to the mirror, marveling at the way the dress made her glow.

Tilting her chin, she covered her face with the modesty veil. And then, humming the "Blue Danube," she began to dance.

She held out her arms to an invisible partner—allowing herself to let him become Derek, just for the fantasy, she told herself—and glided between the bed and the dressing table, smiling as she hummed in her clear, light voice.

"La, da, da da," she sang, remembering how he had held her, how his deep voice had murmured, "This room is made for waltzing."

She dipped to the silent music and basked in the reverie of her unfolding daydream. What would it be like, to dance in a gown like this on your wedding night? To smile at your bridegroom and know that he was yours, finally and forever? And afterward, when the guests were gone and there was rice in your hair and adoration on his face, oh, what would it be like?

When he touched your naked body, with his wedding ring glinting in the moonlight, and made love to you for the first time as your husband?

Oh, what would it be like?

To be married to Derek?

"Stop this!" she said aloud, standing still. "Just stop it!"

"Oh, no, Amy, don't stop," said a voice behind her. It was Derek.

Startled, she whirled around. In the face of reality, the music and the fantasies vanished.

And in their place, Derek towered in the doorway. He was wearing a formal black dinner suit, and the evening fog swirled around him like a huge, flapping cloak. Behind him, the sun was dipping into the Atlantic and the sky had caught fire. Streaks of scarlet and orange flared like torch flames behind him.

"Oh," Amy murmured, moved to tears by the beauty of the moment.

He didn't say anything, only walked into the room and shut and locked the door in one practiced motion. Then he flicked off the light. The room sank into darkness, illuminated only by a muted glow from the bedside lamp.

Amy caught her breath as she saw the look on his face, and turned away.

And viewed in the mirror, through the bridal veil, his expression was reflected on her face . . . an expression of longing, yearning, desire . . .

As she watched, Derek walked up behind her and grazed the fingertips of her right hand with his. The tips only, as if he scarcely dared touch her, as if she would vanish into the night, or shatter into a million pieces of starlight.

With a will of their own, her small fingers closed around his.

Their gazes caught in the mirror, held.

At last Derek spoke. There were tears in his eyes as he turned her to face him, clasping her fingers tightly. "Amy, forgive me, but I can't go on acting anymore. I'm probably throwing it all away by confessing, but I can't help myself. I don't want to be your friend."

Dread flooded through her, followed by the humiliation of being rejected by him. "N-no?"

"No." He swallowed. "I want to be your lover. I love you." His voice was husky with emotion. "And I want you to love me."

Six

"Derek . . ." Amy was so overcome she couldn't speak. Adrenaline poured into her blood; she stopped breathing; her heart raced. In the mirror, she saw herself gaping in shock. He *loved* her? He loved *her*?

Swaying, she stared at him in awe. Her fingers gripped his. The room revolved slowly around them. He seemed to grow taller, until she was bending backward to look at him. She felt as if she were tumbling through time from the highest mountain in the universe, and she reached out her arms to steady herself. Oh, did he really love her? Did he?

He caught and held her, lifting the wispy veil from her face. "Amy, please. Say something. Am I in this all alone? Am I going to die inside? Have I ruined it?"

Love poured into her heart as they looked at each other, each with searching eyes, hoping to find what was already there. It was the timeless moment when lovers first surrender to each other—as Tristan submitted to Isolde, as Lancelot and Guinevere surrendered, as Geneva and her Basil first sealed their love.

"Amy, are you so unhappy you can't speak?" he asked brokenly.

She felt the tears welling in her eyes as she shook her head. "No, Derek. I—I love you too. I can admit it now. I didn't want to. I thought I was being foolish, living in a fantasy world, the way so many other women must. But I couldn't help it. I just couldn't stop myself from falling in love with you."

His face was the sun. "Ah, my love." He nestled her against his chest and rocked her, running his lips over the feverish skin of her brow. "My dearest Amy love."

Time stopped for them. Though the world hurtled on, they stood in the eternal eye of the storm of life, that safe haven that is love, embracing, the bond sealed between their hearts.

"Can you really care for me?" she asked as more crystal tears dampened her cheeks.

"Hush, sweeting, don't cry." He touched the corner of her eye at the same time that a twin tear spilled down his cheek. "Hush, my darling."

He kissed her cheek, her forehead, the bridge of her nose. The caresses of his mouth were like whispered love words as he brushed them over her skin. He cradled the back of her head in his palms as if she were a rare and precious creature, lifting her lips to his to melt them with one single, gentle, perfect kiss.

He smiled. "What are you thinking?"

"That you haven't dissolved into thin air," she said, clearly astonished. "That you're still here and I'm not dreaming."

"I'm here, Amy. And I love you."

"And I love you."

In the distance, the foghorn from another ship called mournfully. The *Meg* replied. Then all was still again, save for the sound of their breathing as they gloried in the sight of each other and the confession of their love.

Derek brought both her hands to his mouth and turned them over, kissing the insides of her wrists and then the backs; and as he gripped them tightly, he sank to his knees before her.

She bent over him and ran her hands through his hair, soft as ermine, panther-black. Like a child, he rested his head against her stomach, encircling her with his arms.

"Oh, Amy, Amy," he whispered. Then he rose, bringing her body up with him. Holding her above his head, he moved in a slow circle, as if they were dancing in a ballet. She looked down on him, her heart welling with love for him, and she knew that tonight she would give herself to him and he to her, and that their lovemaking would be the most beautiful thing on earth.

"There should be candles," he said, "and a summer breeze scented with lavender."

"There are, Derek," she replied huskily. "There are."

Slowly he set her down, then drew the fragile gown off her shoulders, moaning deep in his throat when the creamy, warm flesh was exposed to his view. Together they eased the sleeves off, and her freed arms fluttered around his neck like butterflies released from their cocoons.

Smiling radiantly, he finessed the bodice around her hips, murmuring "ah," when he saw her filmy white camisole and the hardening berries of her nipples thrust against the thin material.

"You're the most beautiful woman in the world," he whispered.

She was rosy with the flush of awakened desire. Stepping out of Mrs. Bordon's gown, she held out her arms to him, ignoring her wave of shyness as her white tap pants, white garters with pink rosettes, and seamed nylons were displayed for his pleasure. "Yes, tonight I am."

"Not just tonight." He embraced her, running

his hands over her back. His fingertips pressed into the soft swell of her bottom. "Always."

Always. A chill iced her blood. Was that a word for the two of them? Or was "tonight" their word? And tomorrow, and tomorrow? For in four days, they would land in England. . . .

"Are you cold, my love?" he asked, hugging her tightly. "Let me warm you."

"Wait." She began to panic. What was she doing? Had she fallen under his magic spell? Fears rose up in waves. She had to stop or she was going to be hurt.

"Here, I'll help."

Derek had misinterpreted her hesitation. As she watched, her arms crossed protectively, he gathered up the wedding gown and draped it across the dressing table. Then he hung the veil over the mirror, and Amy saw herself through it: ghostly pale, a small woman in seductive lingerie . . . and behind her an exquisite man, beaming at her with more love than she had ever seen on the face of another person.

"Derek, I'm afraid," she said in a rush, reaching her arms around his broad shoulders.

He rocked her gently. "No need to be, Amy. No need."

"I don't know . . ."

"Shh. Tonight there are no doubts or fears. Tonight is for us, darling. To love and be loved. Look at me. What do you see?"

She blushed. "A man."

"What else?"

"Nothing." She lowered her gaze. "That's all I see."

He lifted her chin. "You see more than that. You see love. You see desire. Amy, I want you more than I've ever wanted anyone. You know that. You see that in my eyes. And I see the same thing in yours."

"Do you? Derek, do you?"

Lifting her in his strong arms, he carried her to the bed. It was a journey of a thousand heartbeats, a million rays of moonlight, an infinity of kisses. He pulled away the bedspread before he lay her down on cool, crisp sheets, and his hair was ringed with the glow from the lamp. He looked like the most beautiful of angels, the Fallen One, rising from his kingdom to take her soul and make her his.

"Yes, I do see the same thing in your eyes. You really love me. You love me enough."

"Enough for what?"

He trailed a finger down the side of her face and curled her shiny yellow hair around it. "Enough to waltz with me."

Sitting on the bed, he leaned over and kissed her, a long and lingering kiss, a pavane of lips and sighs and the rhythms of the heart. His mouth was sweet as brandy, his breath spicy, like wine. He was a delight to all her senses—the taste of him; the sound of his voice; the sight of his handsome, splendid body; his touch, oh, his touch . . .

And oh, the joy of feeling him, with his hard muscles of buffed copper, his satin-soft lips, the furry hairs of his brows, and butterfly wings of eyelashes. Tentatively she touched all these places, and more, rolling his earlobe between her fingers, running her hand over his straight nose. And he sat statue-still, allowing her fingers to roam where they would, as if she were a blind woman learning his features.

"I love your hands on me," he said in a gravelly voice. His eyes glittered. "I've lain awake nights, dreaming of this moment."

"Me too," she admitted, breathing in his musky scent, savoring the warmth of his body.

"Oh, beautiful, beautiful one," he whispered feelingly, catching her hands and pressing them between his chin and shoulder. "You're my life's blessing."

Then he rose and began to undress.

First he unlaced and removed his black patent-leather shoes and peeled off his socks, standing on one foot with perfect balance, his back curved in a graceful arch like a single pine branch in a formal Japanese flower arrangement. His unruly hair caught highlights of blue as he straightened, his bare feet on the carpet a promise of further intimacies to come.

She raised herself on her elbows to watch as he untied his bow tie and tossed it carelessly on the nightstand, then slid off his jacket. His suspenders accentuated the breadth of his chest, and his biceps flexed as he eased them off his shoulders. Then he started unbuttoning his shirt.

His gaze never wavered from her face as he took off his clothes. He snaked his shirt down his arms. As he pulled it off, thrusting forward his chest, his pectorals and triceps flexed and his abdomen tightened. Carelessly he dropped it to the floor, his eyes flashing as they swept over her, and his thumbs looped around the thin straps of his undershirt.

Then he paused. "Will you take this off for me, sweetheart?" he asked huskily, sinking beside her on the bed.

She nodded. With trembling fingers, she touched the warm, burnished skin of his shoulders. A shudder of desire vibrated through her and she gathered up the cotton fabric hurriedly, eager to be rid of it.

She rose on her knees to pull it over his head, and as she did so, he crushed her against his bare chest and buried his face between her breasts.

"Oh!" she cried, branded by the heat of his mouth. Her camisole stretched like a second skin over the firm mounds of her breasts, delineating their feminine shape and size and the petite points of her nipples. He moved his face between them, breathing in deeply, as his hands gripped her shoulders.

Then he lay her down on the bed and pulled the lacy straps over her upper arms. He looked down at her for a moment, surveying his domain, then claimed her neck and chest for his own with his hands and his mouth until Amy gasped with pleasure.

Her hair streamed over the pillow. As she raised up to kiss him, it fell behind her like a waterfall of liquid gold. When she moved, the light danced and glimmered in the curls, merging with the flecks in his raven eyes. As he moved lower to the first soft swells of her chest, she flashed white-hot, melting beneath him.

She cried out when he cupped her breasts in his large hands, then lowered his lips to encircle each taut center through the fine material. She began to tingle almost painfully, the sensations spreading through her like molten metal.

Derek sighed against her breast. "Ah, my love. I can't wait to undress you. I'm driving myself crazy."

"You're driving me crazy too," she said, then reddened at how gauche that sounded. Those were not the words of romance, but of her everyday life and her tendency to speak first and think later. They were not moonlight words, the murmurings of seduction—the kinds of things Derek whispered to her that made her spine ripple with anticipation.

Derek chuckled. "All right, then, Pleased van Teiler."

He released her and unhooked his black silk cummerbund. She heard the sound of his zipper, the creak of the bed as he stood and pulled his trousers and underwear down his legs.

"Oh, Derek," she whispered.

His nakedness was beautiful. She had never seen a man so exquisite. Lines and angles met in sculpted proportions to create male perfection as his body tapered from his full chest matted with hair to the narrowness of his waist and hips. His thighs were large, the muscles outlined by the lamplight, his legs long and sturdy and tan.

And between his legs rose the pride of his body, his manhood, a thing of splendor and power. A soaring thrill shot through her when her mind jumped ahead to a vision of their lovemaking, when he would join his flesh with hers and fill her with his glory.

She opened her arms. "Derek, please. I want you."

He didn't move. He only looked at her. Slowly she lowered her hands.

"Derek?" she asked in a hesitant whisper.

"By heaven, but you're lovely," he said softly. "It's impossible to believe you're real."

Then he came to the bed. His weight made the mattress dip, and she inclined toward him, pressing her hand against his chest. She ran her fingers through the hair and found the flat nubs of his nipples. He caught his breath and his lids flickered. Emboldened by his response, she rolled them between her fingers and watched in gratified fascination as they hardened and grew.

"You enchantress," he moaned.

He combed her hair with his fingers and smiled. Then, as he studied her face, the smile faded and a look of raw yearning took its place.

Wordlessly, he slipped the camisole over her head, urging her to raise her arms. The material sighed past her ears; she looked through it to see fire blaze in Derek's eyes at the sight of her unclothed body. She pleased him. She swallowed hard. She was so glad.

Once she was free of the camisole, she held out her arms to Derek again. And this time he answered her call, embracing her tightly and lifting her off the bed. Her head fell back, and he kissed her slender, arched neck with a passion that startled her. She looked up at him for reassurance, but his lips trailed down to her shoulders and then to her breasts. He fondled them with hot-blooded hands, sucked and teased them with demanding lips and a tongue like a sizzling dagger.

"It hurts," she said gasping. "It feels so good it hurts."

He said nothing, only drew a line with his tongue down the center of her chest and circled her navel as he pulled down her silken panties.

"Amy," he said raspily, touching the delicate golden triangle between her legs.

Her body erupted into a flash fire of delight. She arched off the mattress, her flesh instinctively seeking his. But he held her down with the force of his gaze and drew the panties over her tensed thighs and calves and pointed toes. She was clad only in her stockings and garters, and Derek left them on.

He fondled her womanhood with knowing, expert hands, probing, finally physically holding her down as she began to writhe. An uncontrollable force built inside her, demanding release, yet everything Derek did intensified it until she flamed like a huge fiery orange sun. She was no longer of the earth; she was of the universe, all the stars and comets shattering one after another into nothingness, until she became the gold in Derek's eyes, which glowed with wonder at the splendor of her fulfillment.

Amy's lids shut, and she succumbed to the thundering ecstasy that galloped through her. And when she came to herself, rising from the haze of rapture, descending from the pinnacle, she saw that she was clinging to him, her fingers digging into his arms.

He shook with desire, and yet he held himself back. Slowly he began to build the flames in her again. *Impossible!* she wanted to tell him.

But Derek knew special ways. His caresses over her breasts and thighs were a powerful aphrodisiac; and when he stroked her with his fingers once again she was astounded to find herself as aroused as before.

"Oh, Derek!" she cried, reaching for him. She wrapped her hand around the rigid fullness of his manhood and moved up and down until Derek, panting, eyes half-closed, pulled away. Then she lay back, enticing him, the flush of sexual desire evaporating her restraint, making her wanton.

"Oh, Amy!" he cried, and plunged into her.

All other sensations paled in the intensity of her joy as Derek joined himself to her. She was so hot, she felt as if her hair had caught fire. Perspiration broke across her chest and forehead and between her legs, where he reared and plunged like a stallion.

He took her, filled her, made her something more than she had ever been, something supernatural—the essence of Woman, mating with Man, merging as one soul over ages and eons.

Soul mates.

Then she floated high above the moon and the rushes of clouds; she imagined she could look down and see Derek inside her, drained, his head resting next to hers. Though her eyes were closed, she saw the rock-hard spheres of his buttocks and the sheen of sweat on the small of his back. She saw her hands entwined in his seal-black hair . . . and she saw the tears that streamed down her face.

"Don't cry, my darling," Derek said soothingly before he kissed her wet cheeks. "Don't."

"I can't help it," she said against his neck. "Nothing like this has ever happened to me."

"Nor to me."

She opened her eyes and smiled tentatively. "Really?"

He frowned. "Of course not. What do you think?"

Before she could answer, her lids drooped shut. She was bone-weary. But in her dozing, she felt Derek roll over and pull her into the crook of his arm, cuddling her.

Yet her heart still pounded in her chest. She had just made love to Derek Morgan. She had sealed herself to a man renowned for chasing women down and capturing them in his bed.

He said he loved her. What did she think?

She didn't know.

"Amy, love? Are you asleep?" Derek asked softly.

They were lying in her bed, the sheet tangled between them. Outside the dawn was breaking and Derek swore he could hear songbirds singing; but of course they were still at sea, and the singing was inside him, in his head and his heart.

"Amy?" he repeated.

Immediately her eyes flew open. "I haven't slept all night," she told him.

Derek's heart swelled inside his chest as he combed her tousled hair with his fingers. Her skin was radiant from their lovemaking—after the first time, there had been a second time, and a third—and her lids heavy with the sleep she denied she'd had. As the hours had passed, he'd watched over her as she dreamed, a sweet half-smile on her lips, and only when he'd kissed her cheek had she roused.

But he truly had not slept. He was too euphoric. He was too much in love.

"Let's talk some more," he said after a long, lingering kiss. "I want to know everything about you."

She snuggled against his bare chest. "We've talked so much, I'm hoarse."

He laughed. "Me, too. And now I know your favorite color is blue and your birthday is in March, and you want your sister's approval and your aunt's murder—"

She made a face. "Derek, please!"

"Well, it's all true, isn't it?" He grinned at her. "Isn't it?"

She traced a heart on his chest and kissed the center of it. "Some of it."

"All."

"Norma did the best she could."

"Right. Such as telling you you were mentally retarded and putting you in remedial classes at school. When all along you were, what did you call it?"

"Gifted," Amy said, "but—"

"Thank God for that sister of yours, who knocked some sense into you. I can see why you care about her so much."

"She's special," Amy agreed.

"And your aunt is a harridan."

"Well, I'm trying to put all that behind me."

"Bravo, my brave girl. But that doesn't stop you from hating Auntie Norma."

"I don't hate her!" Amy insisted.

"Disliking her strongly, then." He lifted her chin and narrowed his eyes as he studied her. "I'm right, aren't I?"

She thrust forward her lower lip, pouting like a little girl. "I think you know me too well already, Mr. Morgan."

"Never. I will never know you too well." He kissed her petulant mouth, his chest tightening as her warm lips became soft and pliant and her arms came around his neck. This woman truly loved him. He could sense it with his heart and soul, and it was a miracle to him that two people could meet and fall in love so fully, so completely, in such a short time. The very idea thrilled him.

"Talk. Talk to me," he said huskily. "I want to soak you up like a sponge."

She laughed. "Derek! I can't talk anymore." She thought for a moment. "But I'll dance for you."

Before he could speak she leaped off the bed and hurried to the closet. She was as lithe as a gazelle; his eyes savored her small buttocks and breasts, delighted in her trim thighs and lovely long neck. In the soft light, her hair bobbed and curled around her head like a gossamer lion's mane.

"Here we go. I'll be right back," she said excitedly, disappearing into the bathroom with something large and heavy wrapped in a dry-cleaning bag.

Derek smiled at the closed door and leaned against the headboard. Life with Amy—and there must be a life with her, or there was no life at all for him—would always be interesting, to say the least. The two of them would keep each other entertained for centuries.

He dozed off and didn't realize it until she brushed his hand and whispered, "Ta-dah!"

Before him stood a wraith from the age of Good Queen Bess. She was dressed in a beautiful velvet gown the color of sable, the sleeves slashed with black and white, and a gold-and-black stomacher running from the bodice to the waist. The starched lace ruff that encircled the back of her neck was dotted with brown "jewels," the stiff lace repeated in a heart-shaped cap.

"You're . . . exquisite," he said, breathless. His throat was tight, and the words came out with difficulty. "You look like Anne Boleyn."

Amy sat down beside him. "Queen Elizabeth's mother?" she asked, horrified. "Oh, please, she lost her head!" She clutched her neck melodramatically. "This be not fodder for the executioner's axe, milord!"

"Thou art right, mistress mine," he whispered, gathering her up in his arms. Her skirts rustled as she moved, her back held rigid by the corset beneath her gown. The low, square bodice pressed her breasts together and lifted them up in the traditional Elizabethan manner. He supposed it was the Briton in him that found her outfit so arousing. "That neck was made only for kissing."

He nibbled her satiny earlobe, then trailed below her jawline with his tongue.

"And these breasts were made for adoring," he murmured, and plunged his face in her scented, sweet softness.

"Oh, Derek," she said, sighing. "Oh, my love."

Derek's heart filled with her words and he gazed up at her; she was blushing prettily.

"I love to hear you say my name," he told her. "I love to hear you call me your love."

He shifted his weight and faced her, lacing his fingers through hers. Then he recited a poem by John Donne that he now realized he had never really understood before:

> *"Twice or thrice had I loved thee*
> *Before I knew thy face or name;*
> *So in a voice, so in a shapeless flame . . ."*

He trailed off, lost in Amy's sparkling eyes. They sat together in happy silence, gazing at each other.

"Let me dance for you," she said at last, and glided away from him.

She reached into a little bag slung on her hip and pulled out two ribbons threaded with tiny brass bells. Quickly she tied them around her wrists and lifted her forearms in front of her face. Then she began to move and sing, a vibrant, living echo of the past—and a promise of the future.

> *"Anon, I am the Queen of Love!*
> *I reign o'er all the world!*
> *God 'ild my loyal subjects*
> *from evil, harm, and ill!"*

Delighted, Derek rose from the bed. "I know that one!" he cried.

Winding the sheet around himself, he fashioned a toga of sorts, singing the verses as Amy marked the steps of the intricate folk dance. When he reached her side, she handed him a second pair of bells, and he tied them on his wrists, shaking them in time to the music in the timeworn pattern: twice in front, twice above, twice crossed, then crossed again.

They touched wrists and moved in a circle, then changed directions. He serenaded her:

> *"And I, I am her Grace's lord!*
> *I rule the Queen of Love!*
> *I alone can rule her heart*
> *and all her power prove!"*

"I didn't know that verse!" Amy said as they began to move faster.

"That's because you're the queen," he replied, "not the king."

"We didn't have a king of love in our traveling fair. Just a queen."

Derek stole a kiss as they crossed wrists. "High time you did, then." He brushed her lips again. "Am I your king, my love?"

For answer, she swept a low curtsy, breaking the rhythm of the dance. But Derek's heart kept tempo, and as he raised her up, his entire being sang with joy.

"I dreamed of you just like this," he told her as he kissed her fingertips and folded her hands beneath his chin. "In almost this exact dress, too. Do you think I was seeing into the future?"

To his surprise, a cloud passed over her face. "Can you see the future?" she asked. "Can you see if . . . ?"

He was taken aback by her abrupt change in mood. "Can I see if what, my love?"

"Nothing." She looked away, then back again. "We missed the cocktail party."

He chuckled. "I'm desolate over it, too."

"But it's very bad manners. If the captain invites you to something, you're supposed to go, no matter what."

She looked so earnest he wanted to laugh, but held himself in check. After all, Amy was not used to celebrity status, or to cruising on luxury ships. Once or twice he had caught her faltering at the dinner table, unsure which fork to use, and his heart had gone out to her. Such concerns had been foreign to him, too, until he hit the big time. He had almost forgotten the hours he had spent poring over etiquette books and being drilled by a studio public-relations woman. And when he had been presented to the Queen, he had nearly died of nervousness.

"I'll apologize to him personally," Derek assured her. "I think he'll forgive me one lapse. And even if he doesn't, I wouldn't have gone for the world." He clasped her tiny waist and held her away, content just to look at her in her astonishing gown. "Not for anything."

"Not even for the chance to play James Bond?" she asked, her eyes twinkling mischievously.

He pretended to consider, then laughed as her face fell. "Not for Bond and not for Hamlet!" he cried, twirling her in a circle.

He spun her around, rejoicing in her laughter as

she threw back her head, her arms straight out to the sides. Had they danced together before in the court of a king? Had she been his lady, his life, his wife?

" 'Did my heart love till now?' " he murmured, so low he wasn't sure she heard him. "Have I loved you always? Was I born to be your soul mate?"

Her small hands wrapped around her shoulders. Her laughter tinkled like the bells around their wrists. "Derek, put me down! You're making me dizzy!"

"Yes, milady," he said, obeying at once. "I shall put you down."

But he would never let her go.

They made love again. Amy couldn't imagine how Derek summoned the energy. She herself was exhausted, and hungry, too. But when he put his hands on her nude body and entered her, slowly and gently, she forgot her hunger and her tiredness and gave herself to the joy of being his entirely. Never in her life had she imagined such exquisite sensations were possible, never such happiness, such fulfillment. It was like a dream. . . .

As Derek moved inside her, she frowned to herself. Too much of this was like a dream. What would she do if she had to wake up?

Derek must have sensed her turmoil, for he stopped thrusting and looked at her questioningly.

"Love, am I hurting you?" he asked, concern in his tone.

She smiled at him and entwined her hands behind his neck. "No," she told him.

"Good." He began to make love to her again.

But *would* he hurt her? she wondered. Oh, would he?

Seven

Around noon, Derek and Amy rose from their bed of love and reluctantly parted so Derek could change into daytime clothes. Amy showered quickly and hurriedly dressed in wool pleated slacks, a crepe de Chine blouse, and a baggy "Hemingway" sweater of teal and gray. She brushed her hair over her shoulders and added a snug gray cap, then made her way down the promenade toward Derek's stateroom, where they had agreed to reunite.

As she walked, she felt excited and tingly inside in anticipation of seeing his room. He had one of the four plush suites on board; that in itself would be reason enough to look forward to seeing it, but on the *Meg* this was Derek's home, and she was going to observe him in his most intimate surroundings—slippers by the bed, razor in the bathroom, maybe a paperback on the nightstand. What did he read? What kind of music did he like? Did he believe in UFOs? There was so much she didn't know about him!

A chill invaded her warmth. There were only three days left before they landed in Southampton. The thought of landing made her queasy; everything was so perfect here on board. They were protected from life's realities, as she had once been protected by Claire and then by college. They had no responsibilities, no jobs, nothing to do but play the mystery game and explore the mysteries of love. What would happen when the real world intruded upon them?

More to the point—would they even have a relationship in the real world? Derek said he loved her, but what did that mean exactly? Was he speaking of a commitment to her? Was he planning to see more of her in London?

Sighing, she huddled in her cardigan as she slowed her steps. In the night and the rosy dawn, with Derek beside her, she had believed in the vision of a love strong and true between a dancing princess and a tall, dark champion. But now, alone in the bright sunlight, she couldn't believe as firmly. Perhaps she had dreamed of their lovemaking. Perhaps Derek really was the ghost of an Irish poet, roaming the decks of the *Meg* for all time. . . .

The door to Derek's suite was reachable only by a small stairway. As she began to climb it, the door opened and an incredibly beautiful redhead dressed in a lemon-yellow jump suit posed on the threshold. She was tying the belt and adjusting the waistband as if she'd just gotten dressed, and her head was thrown back as she laughed merrily.

"Well, that was brilliant, using her like that," she said into the room. "It should take the heat off."

Amy froze on the stairs. Derek said something to the redhead in reply, but his words were lost in the wind.

"Well, call me if you want me." The redhead shut the door and turned to see Amy on the stairs. "Oh, hello," she greeted her breezily. "You must be Amy van Teiler."

Using her? Using whom? As Amy summoned up

a weak smile, the redhead glanced down at the bodice of her jump suit and made a little face. The top of a lacy oyster-colored bra was showing.

"I always miss one," she said, fastening a button. "I should just throw this thing out. It takes so long to put it on again! Well, everything should be okay now," she went on. "I told Derek about the counter-thief and he's ready to go for it." She grinned. "Mystery parties make strange bedfellows of us all, don't they? Oh, golly, I'm late for my massage. See you."

Amy watched the woman trip past her down the stairs and jauntily swing her hips as she headed in the direction of the ship's spa. A knot formed in Amy's stomach, and she drew the edges of the oversized sweater around her, hunching defensively against the gnawing suspicions forming in her mind.

Derek had made love to that woman.

Derek had been using her, Amy, for some purpose.

Derek . . .

"Honestly, I'm ashamed of you," she muttered to herself. "How can you think things like that about him? He said he loved you. Don't you trust him?"

But when she knocked on the door and he answered it, the look on his face did little to allay her uneasiness. At the sight of her, a guilty look flashed over his features, replaced an instant too late by pleasure.

"I didn't expect you so soon," he told her, pecking her cheek before he stood aside to let her pass. Then, when she walked in, he strode ahead of her to the bed, where he lifted the gold-and-black spread over the bedclothes and fluffed the pillows with a furtive air.

"Sorry if I surprised you," Amy murmured, swallowing. The stewards made their beds every morning, so it was highly unusual for Derek to be making his own—unless he had recently been in it.

"Not at all, sweeting." Derek straightened from the bed and made a sweeping gesture. "Well, what do you think?"

The room was nothing short of grand. Decorated in high Art Deco, its walls were papered with orange-and-gold Oriental fans, highlighted by triangular sconces of gold and silver. All the furniture was made of black lacquer, upholstered in various warm-hued brocades to blend with the wallpaper.

"It's beautiful," Amy told him, her heart turning over as he stood in the center of the dazzling, gaudy room, radiating masculine virility like a Chinese sun king glorying in his power.

"It looks like an opium den," Derek countered, laughing. "The sitting room looks like an Egyptian tomb and the bathroom's done completely in black." He shook his head. "The thirties were unbelievably decadent, don't you think?"

Amy heard little of what he said; she was fascinated by the way he moved, the cadence of his voice, and her own small-minded jealousy. She couldn't help it, she pleaded in her own self-defense, but the very fact that she was feeling so miserable—on so little evidence—worried her.

"Dear heart?" Derek queried, taking her hand. "Is something wrong?"

She nervously licked her lips and looked down at his tanned fingers grasping her own. "Nothing, Derek."

"Rot."

"No, really, it's . . ." She forced a smile to her lips. "It's nothing."

He pursed his lips together, but said nothing. Then he led her to a camel-backed club chair beside a small lacquer table and sat across from her in its mate.

"I have news," he said excitedly. "Do you want to

hear it?" She nodded, and he continued. "Well, you'll never guess what. There's a counter-thief aboard, and he's stolen all our loot!"

He sat back triumphantly and folded his hands, stretching his legs beneath the table and tapping her foot with his own.

"How do you know?" she queried carefully, perversely remembering Loretta Hansen's oyster-colored bra.

"Why, Loretta, of cou—"

He stopped speaking and leaned forward. "Oh, darling, you're not upset because she was here when you arrived, are you? I told her you were my accomplice, and it's all right. In fact she said it was brilliant."

Amy sighed inwardly, regretting her inability to hide her feelings from him. "Of course I'm not upset," she said miserably, knowing her tone and expression gave her away. "What you do in your own room is your business, Derek. I—"

"What utter idiocy!" he cried, grabbing her hands up and kissing them. "Amy, do you think I'm such a lout that I'd make love to one woman while another was on her way to see me?"

Amy winced at the frank way he put it. And yet she must think he *was* a lout or she wouldn't be feeling upset.

But he was a movie star, she argued with herself. A jet-setter. Wasn't that the way such people lived?

"Well, she was putting on her jump suit," she mumbled. She peered at him and saw confusion on his face. "Buttoning up her front and tying her belt."

"Ah." His voice was soft. He closed his eyes and chuckled softly. "I must be the king of circumstantial evidence. First you catch me sneaking out of women's bedrooms and then a woman trots out of *my* bedroom doing up her clothes." He cocked his head, his eyes gleaming with amusement and compassion. "Sweetheart, she used the loo." Amy looked at him. "The bathroom. She had to take her jump suit off to use it."

"Oh." Amy's reply was as small as she felt. Dull red crept up her neck and across her cheeks. "I'm sorry."

He molded her hand against the side of his face and squeezed it with his shoulder. "No need to be, sweet love. It certainly must have looked suspicious."

She fought to ignore the happiness flickering through her and concentrate on the issue at hand. But his fingers were warm and velvety, and what was more, they smelled of her cologne and her flesh. As she inhaled, a thousand memories of their lovemaking surged through her mind and filled her heart. Lying in his arms, captured by the brilliance of his eyes and the strength of her desire, nothing in the world had mattered. Nothing else had existed. And now it seemed too good really to have happened.

"It shouldn't be important that it looked suspicious," she said suddenly, fiercely.

Derek rose from his chair and knelt on the floor beside her. He gathered up handfuls of her hair and released them. They floated like clouds of spun gold back onto her shoulders. "For my part, I'm rather pleased you were jealous," he said, nuzzling her ear.

"I'm not."

Besides, she didn't have the right to be jealous, she told herself. It was unfair of her to expect anything from him. After all, Derek had made no promises to her. And she knew that for him, sex in and of itself didn't imply a meaningful relationship. Why, the magazines were rife with stories of his many brief affairs and one-night stands.

And she was probably just one more story to be added to the others.

Derek lifted her mouth to meet his. His kiss was soft, gentle, reassuring, as he rolled his dry lips over hers, brushing the corners as if willing her tension to dissolve. He smoothed the hollow beneath her cheek, the high ridge beneath her eye, her temple. He pressed his head against hers and put his arms around her, rocking her, moaning happily when at last she wrapped her hand around his wrist and squeezed it.

"Let me tell you about the counter-thief," he said. "It will tickle you. And I know how much you love to be tickled."

Amy ignored her own sad feelings and sat back in her chair. "All right," she said brightly. "Tell me."

He started to speak, then tilted his head and gazed at her. "Amy, darling, you know I care for you, don't you?"

When she was silent, he took her hand and flattened it over his thundering heart. "You know I love you. Say it, sweet."

At that moment she believed him. There was nothing else to be done: his eyes, his voice, his body were rich with love. But oh, could such a miracle really occur? "You . . . you love me."

"So true. So right." He shifted his weight, rolling back on his heels and holding on to her hands for balance. "Amy, we both know women throw themselves at me all the time." He laughed uneasily. "That sounds so glib. You were right—movie stars are a conceited lot. But it does happen to me."

His eyes took on a faraway look. "Strange. As a boy I was the too-tall, too-thin, hopelessly disgusting-looking lad you always saw standing directly in one of the blaring speakers at dances. Going slowly deaf."

"You?"

He cupped his ear. "Beg pardon?"

"I said . . ." she began, then realized the joke. "Have you ever thought about making a comedy?"

"Oho, but I started in comedy," he said. "In fact, I acted in no fewer than sixteen comedies." He inclined his head with a flourish. "The great Derek Morgan nearly broke his neck doing a pratfall in *Copenhagen Romp*. It was a sterling work. I'm crushed you've never seen it."

"Oh, I, uh—" Amy murmured, flustered.

Derek massaged her palm. "Darling girl, it was never released in the United States. It was not one of the films that made the legend. I acted in Scandinavian sex romps. No, not porno," he said quickly as her mouth fell open. "They used to make these rather bizarre films where lots of women ran around naked and lots of men—that was always me, one of a cast of 'lots'—ran after them and got caught by policemen and ministers and schoolmasters."

"Art mirrors life," she blurted out, and Derek burst out laughing.

"Well, I've seldom gotten caught, actually. Except by you, and I've been entirely innocent of any wrongdoing in every case, haven't I?"

She smiled sheepishly. "Yes. Except when you were supposed to be doing something wrong."

"Which brings me back to the reason for the visit of her with the tight jump suit and small bladder. It appears that one can apply to the Committee to become a 'counter-thief.' In effect, if you stumble across my hidden stash, you can take it."

"That's cheating!"

"*But* such people have to give the Committee clues to their identity, and if I can guess who it is and steal back the loot, I regain my honor. I can still be accused of being the thief while they've got my things, so it doesn't affect the game for the other players. It's to add an extra challenge."

"But don't the counter-thieves know who you are?"

"No. They only have my property. If I'd been the one who'd found it, though, I'd have simply staked out the place and waited for the thief to reappear. That must mean whoever did it doesn't want to end the game."

She understood that sentiment perfectly. "Have you guessed who did it?"

"No, but I'm hoping we can solve the puzzle together. What's that old saying?"

She smiled. "Two heads are better than one?"

"That's it." He grew serious, his eyes boring into her as he studied for a moment, then laid his head on her chest. "And two hearts are better than one, my love. Far, far better."

Instead of looking for the new thief, Derek and Amy made long and glorious love. They wrestled in the throes of their passion, overwhelming each other with the intensity of their need and desire. Exhausted at last, they dozed, slumbering and dreaming pressed thigh to thigh, Derek's hand outlining the curve of Amy's hip.

After an hour, Derek woke. He smiled tenderly at Amy, then reached into the nightstand and pulled out a manila envelope labeled "Dossier."

Beside him, Amy stirred. "Hello, lambkin," he said lovingly, kissing the end of her nose. "Sleep well?"

"I dreamed about you," she told him, a sunrise-pink painting her cheeks. "You know when you showed up at the séance in that highwayman's outfit? I'd dreamed of you wearing it. That's why I looked so shocked."

At this point, believing in the inevitability of their falling in love and accepting the mystical quality of it, Derek felt only mild surprise that she would conjure up a vision of the future.

"And I've dreamed of you a thousand times as well," he said, his body stirring as she smiled up at him. She was the most exquisite woman he'd ever met. Those amber eyes, that golden hair . . . A thrill ran up his spine as he contemplated her beauty.

But if he should lose her . . .

"These are the clues," he said to distract himself. He showed her two photographs, one of a cow and one of a bar of chocolate.

Amy sat up beside him, arranging the sheet over her breasts. "Is this all?" He nodded. "These two pictures are supposed to tell us who the thief is?"

"I'm afraid so."

She took the envelope from him and looked inside it. "No other clues?"

"None I could find. Loretta said they've thrown me a curve, and not to be disappointed if I couldn't figure it out."

Amy's eyes narrowed. "Oh, she did, did she? We'll see about that!"

"Ah, I love a woman with fighting spirit." Derek bussed Amy's cheek. "A clever, beautiful woman," he added, kissing her with each word. "A clever, beautiful, seductive woman. One who is rapidly making me forget about cows and chocolate bars."

"Am I?" she asked happily. She turned to him, putting her arms around his neck. The sheet slipped from her body, revealing shell-pink, love-sensitive nipples that contracted daintily as he pulled her against his chest. His hands sought, and found, the swells of her bottom and fitted them into his palms, amazed at her perfection. Making love, their bodies fit together as if fashioned from the same lump of clay. Their senses of humor dovetailed neatly, they were both imaginative, and they were both sensualists. If the good

Lord Himself had sat Derek down and asked him precisely what he wanted in a woman, he would have asked for Amy.

"Yes, oh, yes, now I have forgotten about cows and chocolates entirely." He eased her mouth open and penetrated the warm, sweet hollow with his tongue. At the answering touch of her tongue, his body reared and stiffened and his head felt as if it would blow off his neck.

"Do you know there are one thousand, two hundred and fifty-seven documented positions in which to make love?" he asked huskily, spreading her legs apart as she crawled onto his lap.

Shaking her head, she ran her nails down his flat belly, and he nearly lost control.

"Three down, one thousand, two hundred and fifty-four to go," she said, taking him into herself; and Derek answered, "Oh, yes, my love. Yes."

That same day after lunch, Mrs. Bordon discovered Derek and Amy in the library, cups of cocoa in their hands as they pored over a huge dictionary and a *Roget's Thesaurus*.

"Whatever are you two doing?" she trilled.

Amy smiled up at her, feeling slightly guilty that she hadn't been spending more time with the generous old lady who had paid her passage to Britain and treated her with affectionate concern.

"Hello, Mrs. B.," Amy said warmly. "We're working on a mystery." She giggled when Derek nudged her.

"Oh, really? What mystery?"

Amy hesitated, not knowing what to say next, when Mara strode in, twirling a long-stemmed red rose between her hands.

"Hello, Derek," Mara said languidly. "Amy," she added as if she'd just noticed Amy standing beside him.

Derek said nothing, only bobbed his head, and Amy found herself the one greeting Mara.

"How are you today?" Amy asked.

Mara inhaled the scent of her rose and held it against her lips as she looked past Amy to Derek. "Has Aunt Geneva asked you about the scene?"

Derek had no chance to reply before Mrs. Bordon explained. "For our amateur theatricals!" she announced. "We always used to put on little plays back in the thirties. And Mara and I were talking, and we thought it would be such a thrill for her to act in a scene with you." She patted her niece's hand. "She's been a little glum on this crossing."

"Over my divorce," Mara said, sighing.

Derek didn't hide his hesitation, and Amy adored him for it. She knew he was thinking of her feelings, and the realization—coupled with the need to prove to him that she wasn't a jealous, possessive woman—prompted her to telegraph her permission with a slight nod. Still he seemed unsure, but turned to Mara and said, "I'd be delighted."

"Oh, wonderful!" Mrs. Bordon crowed. "Now, we'll need to set up a rehearsal. Can you make it, um, say, in an hour?"

Derek frowned. "Rehearsal? But I thought we'd just read our parts cold and—"

"Oh, no," Mrs. Bordon objected. "That's not the way we did it. We had props and costumes and we all memorized our lines. At the very least, you two must have a rehearsal. For a couple hours, perhaps."

Amy immediately regretted having given her consent. If she'd known *that* was required, she wouldn't have been so pliant. For her and Derek, time was precious, and here were Mara and Mrs. Bordon, devouring it without comprehending what they were asking.

Amy glanced at Mara, who smiled back at her triumphantly. Mara, at least, *did* know what she was asking—and was enjoying Amy's chagrin.

"We'll see you in an hour, then," Mara said in a purr, and aunt and niece left the room.

Derek squeezed Amy's hand. "I can still refuse."

Bravely she squeezed back. "No, it's okay. It would please Mrs. Bordon so much."

"Always thinking of others, aren't you, sweet?" He kissed the top of her head.

She smiled weakly. No, she wanted to tell him. She was usually thinking about him.

They spent the rest of the hour examining the two photographs, staring at them through a magnifying glass, holding them up to the light, and turning them upside down, all to no avail. They were no nearer discovering who had stolen Derek's stolen treasure than before.

"I have to go to the rehearsal now," Derek said finally, pointing to his watch. "You're coming with me, aren't you?"

"No," she said resolutely. She wouldn't be able to stand watching Mara flirt with him without revealing her feelings of jealousy, and she didn't want him to see her writhing under the power of the green-eyed monster again. Better, she reasoned, to avoid the entire situation.

"I'd like to continue studying the pictures," she went on, anticipating his objections. "Maybe I'll come up with something."

Derek looked uncertain, but said, "All right, love," and kissed her lightly. "I'll meet you in two hours."

Instead she didn't see Derek again until just before dinner, when Mrs. Bordon called for everyone to assemble in the lounge to watch his and Mara's scene. Amy assumed he had spent the entire afternoon practicing with Mara, and she tried to cheer herself with the knowledge that she had found a speck of evidence in one of the photos that might help them uncover the counter-thief: The chocolate bar was Swiss!

Now, as she waited for the curtains to part on the improvised stage, she smiled at Mrs. Bordon, who said, "Oh, this is the high point of Mara's life! She's talking about writing a magazine article about it!"

"Indeed," Amy replied.

"Yes. Oh, look, they're going to start."

Applause filled the room as the curtains parted.

Mara was standing alone on the stage, her face buried in a handkerchief. She was wearing a long, tea-colored gown with a high lace neck and flounced sleeves.

Then Derek appeared from the wings, elegant in a World War I army officer's uniform, and put his hand on her shoulder.

"Please, darling, love me," he murmured heartbrokenly. "We can get through this. I know it."

"No. You will leave for the war and forget me," Mara said in a wooden voice. "I will become nothing to you."

"That can never be." Derek's voice broke. "Never, my dearest love."

As the sad scene played out, the women in the audience sat spellbound, eyes wet, lips quivering. Amy looked around her, seeing that he had mesmerized them all, making them believe in his unhappiness at being parted from his beloved Mara.

Making believe. A wave of doubt made Amy queasy. Did he really love her, or was it all an act? Though she knew intellectually that he and Mara were only acting, still he held her own emotions in thrall. She was mourning their parting, as the other spectators were, unable to call herself back to reality. If she was affected like this by a mere scene in a play, how could she sort out her feelings for him—and his for her?

And could it really be love she felt for him, if she was forever analyzing his motives?

"Sweeting, don't doubt me," Derek begged Mara.

Mara looked flustered. He was improvising, Amy understood as she responded to the pet name he used for her. She didn't like his using it with Mara. It seemed an invasion of their intimacy.

Mara covered his hand. "No, my love. I shall never doubt you," she intoned, and then they kissed.

The audience said, "Ooh," in a sympathetic voice, then broke into applause. Derek and Mara kept kissing; gently, Derek broke away and urged Mara to face the audience. They bowed, and then the curtains closed in front of them.

"Oh, weren't they splendid?" Mrs. Bordon cooed, clapping vigorously. "One could almost imagine they were truly in love."

"Yes," Amy said evenly. "One could."

"I wish Bobo could have seen it. He's not feeling well," Mrs. Bordon added, a shadow in her tone.

"I'm sorry to hear that. I hope it's nothing serious."

Mrs. Bordon didn't answer. Instead she waved across the room, saying, "Here they come. Mara's radiant, don't you think?"

"Oh, yes," Amy replied. "Very radiant."

And Derek looked tired and uneasy. Was he afraid she'd be jealous again? Her heart went out to him, and all the twinges disappeared.

"Oh, you two were wonderful," Mrs. Bordon proclaimed. "You had me believing that any minute the staff car would pull up and whisk you away to Africa! I felt the same way I felt when Bobo went to France. He looked so trim and handsome in his uniform—just as you did, Mr. Morgan. Thank you so much for indulging an old lady. Imagine, all that came from one hour's rehearsal!"

At her words, a muscle jumped in Derek's cheek. Amy cocked her head. One hour? But he'd been gone all afternoon.

"I think we should have rehearsed more," Mara cut in petulantly.

"Nonsense, dear. You were superb," Mrs. Bordon said. "Well, I'm off to comfort my darling Bobo. I'm afraid he has a touch of the *mal de mer*. Seasickness," she translated.

"You young people will excuse me, I hope? I'm going to eat dinner in our stateroom. I do hate to miss the buffet, but Bobo likes me to read to him when he's ill." She smiled. "I found the most interesting book. It's a clever mystery novel. I'm sure you two would like it," she added, indicating Derek and Amy. "Once again, you both were sensational."

"Thank you," Derek said.

They watched the elderly woman leave the room.

"I hope Mr. Bordon's not too sick," Amy murmured.

Mara laughed. "My uncle? He has the constitution of an ox. If anything kills him, it will be his fondness for good Scotch whiskey."

Derek looked pained. He took Amy's hand and slid it into his pocket. "We should be going now," he said brusquely. "It was a pleasure, Mara."

Mara's startled anger was not well concealed. Her eyes flashed and narrowed before she managed an overbright smile and said, "Yes, it was fun, wasn't it? We'll have to do it again sometime."

"Indeed," Derek said. "Excuse us."

As soon as they were out of earshot, he unbuttoned the top three buttons of his tunic and shook his head. "What an impossible woman. Did you know this is her third divorce?"

"No, I didn't."

"Well, I'm not surprised. What amazes me is how a man could bring himself to marry her in the first place. And no fewer than three have committed that idiotic act." He shuddered melodramatically.

"And yet I seem to recall a certain air of interest on your part the night we met," Amy drawled, enjoying his pique.

"And you must also recall that lasted only until I turned around and saw you."

He frowned when Amy giggled. "What's so funny?"

"I'm just astonished by your acting ability," she told him. "While you were on stage with her, I had no idea you didn't like her at all." She slid him a glance. "In fact, it looked like you really enjoyed kissing her."

"She has no concept of affection," he growled. "Kissing her was like kissing a wax dummy."

"I feel so sorry for you."

He socked her playfully. "Oh, you do, do you? And I thought I'd find you green with jealousy." Touching her cheek, he added, "But as usual, you're perfect in every way. If I pinch myself, will I wake up to find you were a figment of my imagination?"

Amy cleared her throat. "I've often wondered the same thing about you."

He laughed. "We seem too good to be true, don't we?"

She didn't laugh in return. He was voicing her concerns without realizing it, and she wanted badly for him to reassure her that what they had was something solid, something that would last long after they left the *Meg* and resumed their day-to-day living.

"Listen, I need to change," Derek went on, "and then we'll go to the buffet, all right?"

"Okay," Amy said, rallying herself. "And I can tell you about the clue I found in the photograph."

"Capital! You clever girl." He hugged her against his side as they sauntered down a passageway. "I knew you'd solve the puzzle."

She smiled weakly. "I, uh, expected you back this afternoon. I waited in the library."

He made a face as he unlocked the door to his suite. "I know, love, and I'm very sorry. I got cornered by someone and just couldn't get out of it."

She nodded as if she accepted his explanation, but his words didn't ring true. While Derek was a polite, gallant man, he seemed seasoned in the ways of extricating himself from situations that inconvenienced him.

"I am sorry," he said, pushing open the door. His gaze raked Amy as he shut it behind the two of them. With loving arms he gathered her against his chest. "And if you'll give me an hour of your time, I'll prove it."

They made love again, then dressed for the buffet, which was held in the dining room.

Long tables covered in white linen glittered with ice sculptures of the Tower of London and the British lion. Around them were arranged lavish platters of caviar, smoked salmon, prosciutto, and a dozen entrees including Beef Wellington and a Welsh fish pie that made Derek's face light up with recognition. Past platters of vegetables, potatoes, and salads, frothy bowls of bubbling white-chocolate fondue were surrounded with cherries, pineapples, and strawberries for dipping.

"This is wonderful!" Amy said between mouthfuls.

"Just the usual British fare, for which we are so justly famous," Derek replied haughtily, though his eyes twinkled. "You're sure to get a lot of this at the university."

Amy snorted. "Right."

He appraised her. "I wonder about you, Amy. Traveling with the Renaissance fair, acting the thief with me—don't you think you'll find London University too tame? I know I would."

She covered her reaction by reaching for another piece of pineapple and dipping it into white chocolate. "Oh, I don't know, Derek. This job's a real feather in my cap. It'll mean the start of a real career in my field, not just a job here, a job there. Right now I need a firm foundation so I can build my credentials."

"I see."

"I mean, it's fun to work on individual shows and things, but I'm not at a place where I can command much of a salary. No, I need my feet planted firmly on the ground before I can soar with the eagles."

To her surprise, a troubled expression clouded his face. His eyes grew dark, almost black, and the light went completely out of them.

"I understand," he said, and she got the distinct impression that he was disappointed with her reply.

She fretted as she watched him eat, his movements graceful and measured, almost calculated. He seemed to have been probing her with his questions, and she had the feeling she had come out wanting. Perhaps he now assumed she was a dull, bookish girl beneath her fun-loving exterior.

"But I've had a super time aboard the *Meg*," she added hopefully.

Derek's expression didn't change. He set down his plate and took both her hands in his. "Oh, Amy, so have I," he said, and stared into her eyes for a long, long time.

Eight

After the buffet, Derek suggested they find a place to discuss what Amy had discovered in the pictures, and both agreed their rooms were not suitable. It would be too tempting to make love and yet again put aside Derek's responsibilities to the International Society of Mystery Fans.

So they signed in to the Silver Portal, the famed spa on board the *Meg*; undressed in the posh men's and women's dressing rooms and accepted lush terry towels from their respective attendants; and crept into the dry sauna together.

Once inside, Derek slipped the dossier from beneath his towel and laid it on one of the hot wooden benches as he took Amy into his arms.

"This was a marvelous idea for a secret meeting, love, but at the moment I don't much care about Swiss candy bars and milch cows. All I want to do is unpeel that aggravating towel off your body and kiss you from tip to toe."

The sight of his broad, firm chest with its mat of dark hair made her want to confess that that was what she, too, wanted, but she forced herself to warningly tap his arm. "Now, Derek, we promised we'd work on this. We have to discover who the thief is."

"Why?" he asked petulantly. "The others can still guess who I am. It won't spoil their fun."

"But you promised to enter into the spirit of the game," she reminded him, straining to ignore the way the heat curled his ebony hair into shiny ringlets at his temples and across his forehead. In the soft light of the sauna, his body glowed golden, his perfectly shaped muscles bronzed and smooth. His towel was slung low around his hips and his legs were parted, and as he moved, she glimpsed the shadowed treasure there. Beneath her own towel, her body ached for him, her breasts swelling even as her nipples contracted. Goose bumps rose along her arms and thighs, and she pulled in her stomach to cool the warmth rising from her lower abdomen.

"Someone's gone to a great deal of trouble to steal everything from you," she added, her sentence ending in a quaver caused by her mounting desire.

He sighed, running a hand through his curly hair. The light caught the blue highlights, and they seemed to shimmer through his hair, like fish darting through a moonlit lake.

"You're right, of course. Perhaps instead of Lady Sunshine I should call you Madame Conscience."

She smiled at him. "You're making this very hard, Derek."

"No, *you're* making *this* very hard," he riposted, tugging on the edge of his own towel. "Oh, Amy, I want you so much I can't think straight."

Wagging a finger at him, she said, "No, no, Mr. Morgan. Business first, pleasure later. Besides, we'd probably both pass out if we tried to make love in this heat."

"No, we wouldn't," he said, his tone so sure, she

knew he already had made love in a sauna, some-time in his busy life.

"Let's brainstorm, just say anything that comes into our heads."

"I want you."

"A—a Swiss cow," she said unsteadily. "Swiss chocolate animal. Swiss chocolate milk."

"I want you."

"Derek, please. Swiss—"

He wrapped his hand around her bare shoulder. "Cow Switzerland. Yodeling cow. Matterhorn cow." He lifted her damp hair from the nape of her neck and bent to kiss her there.

"Derek," she protested, shivering with delight. "Foreign bovine."

"Ah, European Bessie." He stroked her upper back. "Russian fingers, Roman hands."

"Why can't I ever resist you?" Amy said dreamily, putting her arms around his neck. "You're a bad influence, Errol Flynn."

"It is my continuing delight to corrupt you, little girl," he answered, running his tongue along the side of her neck.

"Swiss cow, swiss cow," she said gasping. "Derek, we must concentrate."

"I *am* concentrating. My entire body is concentrating. If I concentrate any harder, I'll explode."

"Derek, Matterhorn cow."

He showered her with kisses, assaulting her senses. "Amy, let me see your lovely body. Please, love."

"Yodeling milk. Swiss cheese cow. Oh, oh, oh, Derek, stop."

Then there was a sharp rapping on the outer sauna door. Derek and Amy froze.

"Damn!" Derek swore. "It's the middle of the night. Who the hell takes a sauna in the middle of the night?"

Quickly Derek adjusted his towel, slumping

resignedly against the bench and crossing his legs to hide the fullness of his ardor.

"The pictures!" Amy whispered fiercely. In a flash Derek scooped them back into the envelope and sat on them.

"Well, hello," cooed an all-too-familiar voice.

It was Mara.

"Well, hello," Derek shot back. "Fancy meeting you here."

"I'm not alone," Mara said, and just then, Mrs. Bordon breezed through the door.

She was wrapped, as the others were, in a large white towel. Without her makeup, she looked much older.

"Oh," Mrs. Bordon said, flustered. "Hello." She covered her chest with one wrinkled hand. "Mara, perhaps we should come back later."

"No, please," Derek politely insisted. He started to rise, apparently remembered the photographs, and inclined his head instead. "Amy and I should be going soon at any rate. We've been in here for quite a while."

"Yes, you look flushed," Mara said coyly, eyeing the two of them. "Aunt Geneva, sit down. You'll get light-headed if you keep standing."

So saying, Mara plopped down across from Derek and made a great show of arranging her towel around herself.

"Yes, Mrs. B., come sit by me," Amy urged, trying to hide both her disappointment and the fact that her body was still taut with arousal. She glanced at Derek; from the way his legs were tightly crossed, he was experiencing the same difficulty as she.

The four of them sat in awkward silence for a few minutes. Then Mrs. Bordon piped up.

"So did you two solve your mystery in the library today?"

Mrs. Bordon was looking at Amy as she spoke, and so didn't see the look of utter shock that flashed over Derek's features. But the expression disappeared as abruptly as it had appeared, leaving Amy startled and curious. What had caused his reaction?

"Actually, we did," Derek said casually. "It's fascinating how many differences there are between British and American English. We were debating the usage of the word 'napkin.' In England, we say 'serviette.' A napkin is something else entirely." He winked at Amy. "A baby diaper, in fact."

"Well, that *is* fascinating." Mara tucked the errant corner of the terry square between her breasts. "I wonder what interesting language differences you'll find in Australia."

At her words, Derek shifted uneasily and lowered his lashes.

"Oh, are you going to Australia?" Mrs. Bordon asked.

"Indeed he is," Mara answered for him. "Two days after we land in England."

Amy's lips parted. He was leaving? And he hadn't told her?

"I believe you're scheduled to be gone for three months. And then it's Tunisia, isn't it? And after that, Hollywood?"

Derek raised his eyes to Amy's. There was a pleading look on his face that tore at her insides. He wasn't even going to *be* in England after they had landed. All her worries about their relationship were for nothing! All that hoping and daydreaming for nothing.

She swallowed back tears of hurt and humiliation. She felt so foolish, so ridiculous. She had been an idiot to dream there was more to his "love" for her than one of Mrs. Bordon's wonderful, whimsical shipboard romances. She should have realized that "I love you" meant an entirely different thing to him.

But he should have told her, prepared her, warned her!

"I imagine you'll be gone an entire year," Mara pressed on, smoothing her dark hair away from her face.

"Yes," Derek said quietly. He looked at Amy. "I think we've been in here long enough."

"So have I," Mrs. Bordon put in, fanning herself. "I can't take this heat as I once could. Do you know, in the old days the *Meg* didn't have a sauna like this, but she did have—"

"Excuse me," Amy said, leaping up.

She bolted for the door. Outside, the cold air was a second shock, and she teetered for a moment, horribly dizzy. But she regained her balance and ran into the women's dressing room, flinging herself into the shower.

The stream of tepid water mingled with her tears as huge sobs racked her body. Gone for a year! A *year!*

All her fantasies, all her daydreams . . . ashes.

Her heart . . . leaden.

She couldn't believe he hadn't told her. He must know she cared deeply for him. He must realize she wasn't as sophisticated in matters of the heart as he, and that for her, love meant the old-fashioned kind, enduring and faithful.

And Mara! Did she have a heart? How she'd enjoyed dropping each bomb, with the skill and devastating effect of a seasoned fighter pilot, enjoying each agony she inflicted on Amy. Why did she take such pleasure in killing her? She was a devil, a devil!

Amy cried fresh tears, then forced herself to stop when she heard Mrs. Bordon's clear voice as she discussed the situation with her niece.

"Well, to tell you the truth, dear, I rather thought he was smitten with her too. I saw them looking at each other in the library with what seemed like love. But I suppose I'm just a hopeless romantic. Yet it was a cruel blow to deal her, my dear."

"I only did it because I didn't think he had," Mara said defensively. "Honestly, Aunt Geneva. I didn't want her to be any more hurt than she was."

Their voices dropped. Amy stayed in the shower until the other two women showered and left. With shaking hands, she pulled on her own clothes and trudged through the spa to the exit, oblivious of the beauty of her luxurious surroundings.

She half-dreaded, half-hoped that Derek would be waiting beyond the door, but the hallway was deserted. Heavy with sorrow, she wove her way down the corridor, her agony blinding her, until she looked up and realized she was lost.

She raised her hand to her forehead and took a deep breath to calm herself.

Sweet harp music filled the air. Amy shook her head to make the music stop, but a gentle melody filtered through her confusion.

Turning, she saw that she was standing near the entrance of one of the *Meg*'s other bars, the Jungle Room.

"Would you like a table, miss?" a steward asked solicitously.

"No, I . . ." Amy began, and then straightened her shoulders. "Yes," she said in a strangled voice. "In the darkest corner you have."

"Yes, miss," the steward responded, looking concerned.

The bar itself was quite dark, and the booths and tables were separated from one another by frosted-glass partitions etched with gazelles and zebras. She had almost as much privacy as she would have in her own stateroom.

"What would you like?" the man asked gently.

She nodded. "Something strong. I don't really care what it is."

"Very good, miss." He hesitated. "Would you like

to talk to someone? The cruise director, perhaps? The chaplain?"

"No." She bit her lower lip to keep herself from crying. "It's something silly." Throwing back her still-damp hair, she smiled through welling tears. "I'll get over it."

"I hope you do, miss."

He returned a few minutes later with something tall and orange and topped with a little paper umbrella. "A Southampton Tea," he explained. "I think you'll enjoy it."

Before he could leave her table, she took the umbrella out of the drink, drank half the contents, and unsteadily set the glass on the table. "Bring me another, please," she told the startled man.

Amy was vaguely aware that she was staggering down the passageway to her room with three paper umbrellas cradled in her hand.

"I'm in trouble, I'm in trouble," she mumbled, the walls spinning. Their garish orange-and-jade fan patterns waved at her, and she shut her eyes for a moment, struggling to regain her equilibrium.

She had a dim recollection that the solicitous steward had offered to escort her to her cabin, but she had struggled to her feet and gathered her umbrellas with great dignity. "I can manage," she had assured him.

"Can't manage now," she whispered. "Help."

As she spoke, every bone in her body turned to rubber. In slow motion, she began to float toward the floor.

But strong arms caught her before her knees touched—arms she knew and adored, muscular and smelling of dusky sandalwood, that picked her up and carried her easily up to a hard, masculine chest.

"Oh, my little love, I've been searching for you everywhere," Derek said, his voice breaking. "I'm so sorry about what happened."

"Lemme go," she protested, her words slurred, as she struggled to free herself from his embrace. "I c'n manage."

"No, love, I'm afraid you can't," Derek murmured.

To her utter horror, tears flowed down her cheeks. "Please. So embarrassed."

"Don't be embarrassed, my sweet darling. Everything's going to be all right. I promise."

"Hah," she mumbled, closing her eyes.

Damn that woman, damn her, Derek thought as he carried Amy to her stateroom. He could have slapped Mara for her sadistic cruelty. How dare she hurt his precious Amy like that!

Derek had run from the sauna in search of Amy, but the receptionist had told him she was already gone. Like a madman, he had searched the ship, but he had never found her. Now he wondered if the receptionist had made a mistake in telling him Amy had left. What if she had lingered in the spa, waiting to speak to him, and he had never shown?

"Damn her," he said aloud, again seeing Mara's delighted smile as Amy died a thousand deaths in front of the three of them.

On top of everything else, Mara had ruined what should have been one of the most beautiful nights of his life: the starry, moonlit night when he would propose marriage to the woman he adored and cherished.

Carefully adjusting Amy's weight, he unlocked her door with her key and carried her into the room.

It was filled with red roses, hundreds of them, in banks along the walls, white wicker stands, and glittering crystal vases. Derek himself had never seen so many flowers, even at the lavish Hollywood parties and British fetes he'd attended. Against the brilliant field of red, Amy's translucent beauty was even more pronounced, and Derek cursed Mara again for making a shambles of his plans.

Gently he lay Amy on her bed and sat beside her, smoothing her hair over her pillow. She looked like a sleeping princess, Sleeping Beauty, and he wondered if she would awaken with a kiss, as the fairy tale promised. . . .

Closing his eyes, he brushed her mouth with his. She stirred, but did not waken.

Derek decided to let her sleep. Despite the turn the evening had taken—in fact, all the more so because of it—Derek was determined to ask Amy to be his bride before the morning broke. He would not let her suffer by thinking that he had planned to leave her behind without a second thought. As if he could! But she needed to be told that, shown that he wanted to be with her forever and always.

He had to return to his stateroom to finish his plans, and then, perhaps, he would wake her and beg her to make his life complete.

His chest tightened as he gazed down on her, so still, so perfect. In his mind he heard the lilting strains of their waltz together, saw her jewellike eyes as she gazed up at him. How honest she'd been when she confessed he intimidated her! *For one thing, you're very famous. I'm not used to meeting celebrities. You've got to admit you're something to look at.*

Chuckling, he plucked a rose from one of the vases on her nightstand, kissed it, and laid it on her pillow. The petals were as soft as her cheek when he nuzzled it with his nose.

He straightened. "Sleep on, sleeping beauty," he murmured, and crept from the cabin.

*   *   *

For one so tipsy, Amy awoke with an astonishingly clear head. She had no idea how long she'd slept, but she remembered a dream in which Derek had found her weaving down the passageway and carried her to her room, and—

"Oh," she said, gasping. "Am I still dreaming?"

She sat up as she gaped at the huge bouquets of roses. There must have been hundreds of them. Everywhere she looked, the velvet-red blossoms greeted her eyes.

She reached down and touched the one lying on her pillow. All the thorns had been removed.

"Oh, Derek," she whispered, tears following. Was this a peace offering, an apology, or meant to say something more? After all, wicked, womanizing Errol Flynn had once filled Mrs. Bordon's room with flowers too.

As she pondered, inhaling the sweet, heady scent, her door opened and Derek stood in the doorway, dressed in his black thief's clothes. He was carrying a large cardboard box, and he was so pale, he looked like a specter. His eyes burned in his face like twin coals.

He appeared startled. "Oh, you're awake," he said, coming into the room.

She stiffened, but nodded and gestured to the glorious riot of crimson. "Thank you."

As if with one single stride, he reached the bed and knelt beside it. "Forgive me for causing you pain, dear love. I didn't mean to. I—"

"Oh, Derek, it's okay," she said airily, forcing an untroubled expression over her features. "I overreacted in the sauna. But afterward I met a really nice man, and we had drinks in the Jungle Room." Her awkward giggle sounded more like a sob. "I'm afraid I got carried away. By you, as a matter of fact! Thanks for rescuing me."

He regarded her tenderly. "It's lucky for both of us that you're the worst liar in the world," he said musingly. "Otherwise, I might believe you, and we'd spend the rest of our lives clinging to bitter-sweet memories."

"What do you mean?" She looked down and saw the box sitting on the floor. "What's that?"

He hesitated for a moment, the oddest look on his face—she detected uncertainty, eagerness, and was that fear, too? His jaw moved as if he were grinding his molars, and he swallowed hard just before he spoke.

"I stole back the loot," he told her. "I solved the mystery and robbed the other thief."

The mystery game. What fun she had had, playing it with him! The fantasies they'd woven for each other—James Bond and his sidekick, slinking through the night! Had everything been a fantasy? Was that what the flowers meant? That he was sorry the game was over and it was time for both of them to face reality?

Horrified that she would burst into tears in front of him, she managed a brave smile. "You did? Who on earth was it?"

He smiled back. "Name some Swiss cities."

"I . . . I don't know any," she said, puzzled.

"Sure, you do. That famous one, where they signed a document called the Geneva Convention."

"Geneva!" Her mouth fell open.

"And there's a dairy-products company that had a cow as its logo. Remember the Borden cow?"

"Elsie the Borden cow!" Amy cried. "Geneva Bordon! But that's incredible!"

"She's been a double agent all along," he said. "That scene during the séance? She contrived it, for some reason. And I'll bet Mara accidentally foiled her by noticing her missing bracelet under the table—which is probably where Geneva slipped it herself."

He shook his head. "Can you imagine how much fun she's been having, savoring her secret? I'm astonished she didn't give herself away, the way she prattles on sometimes."

"Yes, she does." Amy remembered the conversation she'd overheard in the spa. How mortifying, to know that Mrs. Bordon understood how deeply Amy cared for Derek—and that, apparently, he didn't care as much in return.

"But I think I've recouped everything. Here's my checklist." He took a piece of paper out of his jeans pocket and unfolded it. "Why don't you go through the box and I'll check off the items?"

Oh, couldn't they stop now? she wanted to ask him. Was he going to pretend the scene in the sauna had never happened?

"All right," she said in a raspy tone, accepting the box as he handed it to her.

Her fingers trembled as she held up the first item. "Silver box," she said.

"Check." He nodded.

"Emerald earrings."

"Check."

"Oh, look, here's a loose stone," she said, fishing in the box. "No, it's a ring. A diamond ring. Is it on the list?"

Derek was silent for a long time. Then he put down the paper and took her hands in his. "No, my love, it's not."

Her heart began to hammer. It looked like an *engagement* ring.

Don't be crazy, she warned herself. Don't think crazy things. You'll only be hurt.

"It . . . isn't?" she asked in a shaky voice. She didn't look at him as she spoke. She couldn't. She was thinking wild things, full-blown daydreams . . .

Derek didn't answer. Amy's heart thundered so loudly, she was sure he could hear it. It throbbed against her rib cage like the mighty heart of the *Meg* herself, driving the ship through the waters.

Driving Amy through dangerous shoals of ridiculous assumptions, foolish iceberg images of white lace and church steeples . . .

Derek squeezed her hands tightly. "You know what it is, my love. You know what it means."

Amy saw the tufts of hair on his long fingers and smelled salt and soap as he bent closer to her. She felt a whisper of his breath on her cheek.

"Amy, look at me."

"I . . . can't."

"But my love, why not?"

He cupped her chin with his hand and raised her face to meet his gaze. His dark, piercing eyes bored into her, and she felt very alone: If her heart were about to be broken, she would have no one to turn to. Claire was far away, in California, and she couldn't go to Mrs. Bordon. She would be too humiliated.

"I . . ." She licked her lips. "I'm not sure what's happening here."

The golden flecks in his eyes danced like dust motes before her. "Aren't you?" He took the ring out of her limp hand. "Don't you know what it means when a man offers a ring to a woman?"

She smiled tremulously. "Derek, please."

He locked eyes with her, forbidding her to look away again. "My love, I want you to marry me. I want you to spend your life with me."

His words struck her like lightning bolts. Stupefied, she covered her mouth, and her eyes widened with astonishment. Then tears of happiness sprung up. "You're . . . you want to *marry* me? You want to marry *me*?"

He nodded vigorously. "Yes, yes, my darling. Say yes."

When she said nothing, only stared at him in perplexed joy, he gripped her hand and slipped the ring on her left ring finger, then kissed her palm, and laid her hand against his cheek.

She was dumbstruck. Staring down at the ring, her unfocused eyes seemed to throb with the wildness of her heartbeat. She thought she was going to faint.

"Dammit, Amy, say something!" Derek ran a hand through his hair. "Say yes!"

"You love me," she said slowly. "You really do."

"Of course I love you. I told you I loved you. Didn't you believe me?" He looked despairing. "Don't you believe me now?"

A few seconds passed before she found her voice. "Yes! Yes, I do!"

She flung herself into his arms and they tumbled to the floor. She rained kisses on his head, his temples, easing back his head to shower more on his nose, his cheeks, his parted lips.

She exulted as Derek gave himself up to her celebration of her love for him, then returned it in kind. He held her as if he would never let her go, running his hands over her body again and again as if to assure himself she was real.

Then he grew serious, pressing her palms together between his own—double sets of hands in prayer—and closed his eyes.

When he opened them, he gazed with luminous reverence at her. Her heart swelled; she had never seen a man look at her like that. No one had loved her this much. No one had truly worshiped her before.

When he spoke again, his voice was hushed. "Once I give my heart, it is not mine to take back. Or to share with anyone else but the woman I love. And I love you, Amy darling. Once in love with Amy, always, always in love with Amy."

"Oh, Derek!" She put her mouth over his, her body quickening as he parted his lips and allowed her entry. She kissed him in ways that she had learned pleased him, heating the secret recesses of his mouth—the ridge behind his teeth, the inside of his lip—warming him, fanning flames she knew would burst into wildfires once he reached the melting point.

She had so much to give him, so much! When he was tired, she would hold him. When he was in pain, she would soothe him. When he wanted to be alone, she would guard his privacy with the ferocity of a lioness. And when he wanted her, she would join her flesh with his in delirious abandon.

She combed her hands through his hair and dotted his face with kisses. His smooth, high forehead furrowed with concentration as he gave himself up to her hands and lips.

"I want to cherish you, my forever love, my wife."

Amy smiled joyfully at him. "I do, too, my love." She blushed. "My husband."

They made love then. Triumphant and ecstatic, Derek plunged into Amy, sealing the acknowledged bond between them, losing himself in the new world they were entering together.

He gloried in her nude, aroused body beneath his, her small, perfect breasts, the soft curves of her hips. That such a beauty should love him! It was a miracle.

Her cries of pleasure sent him over the brink and they found their release together. Then, panting and sated, Derek pulled the covers over them and carefully arranged the pillow under her hair.

"You know, you almost caught me with the ring. I was holding the box in my hand when you came to my suite. So I stuffed it under the bedspread and pretended to make the bed. I was so nervous, I was sure you'd think something was up."

She flushed. "I did. Only, I thought it had something to do with Loretta Hansen."

Sighing, he smoothed her hair over the pillow

and gazed at her tenderly. "My poor Amy. I've led you a merry dance, haven't I?"

"As long as you're repentant, I forgive you," she replied, kissing his cheek.

"Oh, I am, I am." He kissed her cheek in return. "Good night, Mrs. Morgan," he murmured. His heart melted at her glowing smile. It lit up the room.

"Good night, Mr. Morgan."

An hour later, Amy woke up sweating from her dreams and sat bolt upright in the bed. Beside her, Derek continued to sleep, peaceful as an angel.

Amy stared down at her hand. All at once panic clutched at her so strongly, she thought she might be ill.

"Oh, my God," she whispered. "What have I done?"

This was the kind of thing the old, irresponsible Amy would do. Imagine, leaving home for a job and marrying a woman-crazy movie star instead! Talk about fulfilling a fantasy!

Amy knew dozens of theater people. Their emotions, while intense, were not long-lasting. Romances blossomed and withered within the time span of a play production, despite the fact that the lovers involved were positive that *this* time, love would endure.

The Elizabethans believed that love was inconstant, that, inevitably, your lover would tire of you and forsake you. It was a natural consequence of an unnatural state.

She and Derek were lost in the first flush of love. Both of their hearts were full, and when that was the case, it was impossible not to believe implicitly in "happily ever after." There was no problem too big, no complication too vexing, that love couldn't solve.

Or so lovers believed.

But was that true life? Weren't there times when love did not conquer all?

Would their love last, or was it a passion of the moment?

She would have to forsake her job if she married him. What would her life be like, traipsing all over the world with him, sitting idly by while he worked? And then, if it ended, where would she be? To have turned down a position at London University, on little, if any, notice, would make it difficult for her to obtain a worthwhile job in the future.

"I don't care," she whispered fiercely. "He does love me. He will always love me!"

But all of a sudden Amy was not so sure.

Nine

It was morning, and Amy's heart still pounded as waves of anxiety washed over her. Twisting the exquisite diamond ring around her finger, she watched Derek sleep. She wanted to wake him up and ask him to kiss away the nagging flurries of panic, but he looked peaceful and content and she was loathe to wake him.

Or to admit that she wasn't sure if they were doing the right thing.

Silently, she dressed and left the cabin. She stood outside in the chill air, watching the sun awaken to warm the day. Blankets of gray clouds transformed into pastel coverlets of mauve and pink, then darkened to red and fuchsia.

That was how love should grow, Amy reflected, her frozen hands clutching the railing. Slowly, almost imperceptibly, until all at once you blinked and saw your friend transformed into your lover. The suddenness of Derek's and her love for each other concerned her—how could it be real, how could it last? Was it mere infatuation? Were they on the verge of making a big mistake?

" 'Marry in haste,' " she said, sighing, " 'repent at leisure.' "

She walked on, the wind whipping her hair, as it had the very first time she laid eyes on Derek. A ghost of a smile crossed her lips—the fan man! The Irish poet. The infamous, roving, Derek Morgan!

Ahead of her stood another figure bundled against the cold. Amy stopped, not wishing to disturb the other person, but the figure turned in her direction and held out a hand.

"Amy, dear," Mrs. Bordon said, not smiling. "I was just thinking about you."

Amy joined Mrs. Bordon beside the rail. "You were?"

Mrs. Bordon nodded. "Bobo told me everything. Is that your engagement ring? Oh, it's lovely!" Her voice did not hold her usual bubbling enthusiasm.

"He . . . told you? But how did he know?"

She gave Amy a conspiratorial glance. "Apparently, it was not seasickness that troubled him yesterday. Your Mr. Morgan and my Basil sat down for a man-to-man talk in the Crow's Nest. Derek wanted Bobo's advice on marriage. They drank nearly an entire bottle of whiskey."

So that was where Derek had been all afternoon. Warmth diffused Amy's chill as she contemplated Derek, so outwardly sure of himself, so commanding, soliciting the opinions of the older man. It gave him a humble, caring quality that endeared him to her.

"What do you think about our getting married?" Amy asked Mrs. Bordon, certain the lady would regale her with proclamations of how wonderful and romantic the situation was.

Instead Mrs. Bordon sighed. "I'm not sure, dear. Oh, I know I dropped a few hints here and there, but I never dreamed he'd actually propose." She paused. "You know, marriage is never an easy road, but to walk down it with a man you hardly know . . ."

"Yet you fell in love at first sight with Mr. B.," Amy pointed out.

"But I didn't marry him right away. I took a long time to get to know his character." An expression of sadness spread over her face. "And still I didn't know him well enough. Bobo . . . has his faults. He doesn't know that I know about his . . . affairs, but I do, Amy."

She touched Amy's cheek. "Marriage rarely changes people, my dear. What a man was before he marries is what he is afterward. It's not as 'happily ever after' as one dreams it might be. When the bloom wears off, and you realize that your knight has a few rust spots on his armor . . ." Her voice trailed off.

"Just be very, very sure about what you're doing, darling girl. I know my niece can be a hurtful woman, but she's been through a lot with her divorces. It's made her quite bitter."

Amy frowned. "This doesn't sound like you at all. You were so into love and romance."

Mrs. Bordon looked sheepish. "With the idea of it, perhaps. Oh, I'm a silly old woman, mixing you up like this! I feel almost responsible for what's happened."

"Mrs. Bordon, I am a grown woman."

"Yes, but somehow untouched. There's an innocence about you that not many girls have these days."

Her expression changed. "Here comes your young man now," she said, and Amy turned around.

How handsome Derek looked, striding into the wind! Her chest tightened with possessive pride.

"Good morning," Derek said cheerily. "Has Amy told you our news?"

Mrs. Bordon smiled brightly. "Yes, indeed. I'm so happy for you both." She held out her hand, and Derek squeezed it.

Then her smile slipped and she looked up at Derek with eyes sharp and hard as steel. "If you ever hurt this dear child, you'll have me to answer to."

Derek's lips parted. He put an arm around Amy's shoulders and drew her close to him. "Geneva, I have no intention of hurting her."

"Good intentions are not enough," Mrs. Bordon snapped, and turned on her heel.

"Good grief, what's gotten into her?" Derek asked as they watched Mrs. Bordon march stiffly down the promenade.

"She's worried about me," Amy said. "Derek, I think we need to talk."

Giving her a hug, he regarded her adoringly. "After breakfast, darling. Come. I've planned a surprise."

"What . . . ?" she asked, but followed behind as he took her hand and climbed flights of steps toward the topmost deck of the ship.

Motioning for her to keep quiet, he led her along the row of lifeboats and bent beside the one in the middle. With the quick, knowledgeable fingers of a sailor he worked the line through the grommets and stretched the coated canvas up high enough for Amy to slither under.

Giggling, she scrambled into the large covered boat, its canvas cover like a tent above her.

"There's a torch just above your head," Derek whispered.

Torch. Flashlight, Amy translated, and felt with her hand. When her fingers closed around the flashlight, she flicked it on.

To find a silver tray holding a coffeepot, cups, croissants, and jam, carefully arranged in the bow.

"Here I come," Derek said quietly, and crawled in after her.

"What is all this?" Amy asked, touching the pot. It was warm.

"Breakfast for two in our nautical tree house," he told her, sprawled on his stomach alongside her as she rested on her elbows. "Isn't this fun?"

She laughed. "You're crazy!"

"All actors are crazy. Pour me a cuppa, love."

She did, then filled her own cup. They clinked them together.

"To a long and happy life together," Derek pronounced.

Amy smiled weakly. "Derek, we should talk."

"May I have a croissant, dear?"

"Derek . . ." He smiled at her expectantly. "Oh, all right." She buttered it and slathered it with jam, took a little taste, and passed it to him.

"How did you manage all this?"

"The steward's a fan of mine. By the way, did you ever figure out why that Spanish fan was a clue?"

"No, I—" she began, but the *Meg* let forth with a foghorn shout. As close as they were to the sound, it startled Amy out of her skin, and she rolled against Derek.

"We've done this before," he whispered.

At once he caught her in his arms and crushed his lips against hers. His fingers dimpled her back as his soft, dry lips pressed against her mouth. She caught her breath and answered his kiss, and Derek flicked the flashlight off. The darkness hid them, but the electricity that crackled between them lit their cavelike retreat with the white light of instantaneous passion.

Alone in the foggy dawn, they clung to each other. Derek opened his mouth and Amy eagerly took it. His groan was silent, a vibration in his throat that throbbed through his body. He was delicious, and she explored the hidden hollows for the places that made him seize and gasp. Their tongues met. She gripped the rock-hard muscles of his arms as they dueled, and reveled in the beauty of his man's body.

"Oh, my beauty. My love. My wife."

Derek buried his face in her hair and grabbed masses of it with his hands. She felt his sighs against her jaw and moved her head in a slow circle. He kissed the nape of her neck and held her when the showers of chills made her shiver.

They didn't speak; they couldn't see. But Amy knew her beloved's face so well, she could imagine the gold in his eyes and the angles of his face as he immersed himself in the erotic sensations. She could see him smile, and then grimace with exquisite agony as their loveplay grew more intense.

And she smelled his man smells—his freshly scrubbed face and hands scented with soap, the sandalwood of his cologne, and the musky, darker odor of desire. She smelled her own floral cologne on his fingertips and closed her eyes with emotion when he slipped one of his fingers into her mouth and she sucked on it.

"I love you," Derek murmured. "I adore you. I cherish you."

He pulled her on top of him. Her breasts flattened against his chest, but the delicate buds of her nipples stiffened almost painfully as she and he caressed each other's faces with their hands and lips. Derek followed the indentation of her cheek with the soft flesh of his nose, then nuzzled her temple. Her body flared in response.

"You're so handsome," she whispered. "Sometimes I think you're a statue of a Greek god come to life. It gives me chills to see you."

Derek caught her hands and brought them to his lips. He sucked on each of her fingers and circled the centers of her palms with his tongue. She reared slightly. He held her, sitting up to kiss her lips.

The foghorn blared again; this time they chuckled together.

Then, just beyond their secret nest, footsteps

echoed on the varnished deck and stopped a few yards from their lifeboat.

"But I love you, *cara*," said a voice, sighing. Amy recognized it as belonging to Giovanni, their waiter.

"Don't be silly. No one ever loves me," came Mara's tart reply.

"I do. I love you. Let me visit you in London."

"G'ianni, you don't have to act like this. You know I've enjoyed sleeping with you."

"It is not an act," Giovanni insisted. "I want to marry you."

"What?" There was tenderness as well as shock in Mara's voice.

"Sì, sì," Giovanni said, and then their footsteps moved on. "We can marry . . ." His voice died in the distance.

"Oh, my," Amy whispered. "What do you think about *that?"*

"This," Derek replied, and pressed his mouth over hers.

The kiss grew more passionate. Derek's tongue was hot and searching, like his manhood, which prodded against her inner thigh. Amy fought not to groan and nearly failed; she licked her lips and moved gently away. Mara's and Giovanni's voices had brought her back to her senses. They couldn't make love here—what had they both been thinking?

But Derek's insistent hands reached for her. Settling his weight over her, he kissed her lips, then pushed up her sweater and wrote with his finger on her stomach.

"ILY."

I love you. She nodded happily, ignoring the churning fears that had kept her awake all night.

"MAKE LOVE."

She paused, then pushed up his sweater and

wrote, "LATER" on his stomach. Before he had a chance to argue, she added, "NOT HERE."

"Y?"

As her answer she let out a huff. Why, indeed! What if someone heard them and came to investigate?

Derek understood. He peeked out, saw the coast was clear, and raced with Amy to his suite, where they fell into bed to make wild love.

Sighing with pleasure, Derek tickled her lovingly under the arm, then wrapped her in his strong embrace. Without a word, they adjusted their positions until each was comfortable, legs and arms tangled like two puppies worn from frolicking in the potent delights of life.

Amy kissed the side of his neck and he squeezed her shoulder. He pressed his lips to her ear and whispered, "I want to tell you how wonderful our lovemaking was."

She laid her head on his chest. "With you, it's always wonderful."

"It was so intense, I thought I was dying."

"Yes."

Closing her eyes, Amy relived each glorious moment, etching their images across her heart. Even now, she could scarcely comprehend the depth of the power and the passion that had forged them together into one undulating, shimmering being. Their lovemaking had been like a religious experience to her.

What greater force in the universe was there than love?

Two hours later, Derek felt a mixture of relief, guilt, and tenderness as he penned a note to Amy and left it on his pillow beside her.

She must have been exhausted, for she slept so heavily, even a gentle nudge failed to wake her.

There were shadows under the heavy fringes of her lashes, and she seemed unusually pale.

He felt relieved that she hadn't awakened, because he was worried that she was having second thoughts about marrying him; and he felt guilty, because he knew she was right. They would have to talk about their hopes and fears, and he had promised to do so—and now he was practically sneaking away from her to postpone it.

But he *did* have to go to a meeting with Loretta Hansen, he reminded himself, and he *did* have a responsibility to the International Society of Mystery Fans, and he *did* have to have a fitting for his costume for the fancy dress ball, to be held that night.

Yet these were still rationalizations. He could have awakened her an hour ago so they could hash things out. But he had been a coward, taking the easy way out.

"Meet me in the library at two o'clock," the note read. "We'll talk. I love you."

But at two he waited in vain for her; he tried again in the lounge during high tea, at four. Still no Amy. He wondered if she was angry with him.

But as he was leaving the lounge, Mrs. Bordon hailed him. "Amy asked me to tell you she's being swamped by people asking her to help with their costumes. She'd like you to meet her in her stateroom to escort her to the party."

He frowned. "Isn't she going to dinner?"

"I guess not."

"Thank you," he said, and set out immediately for Amy's room.

But she wasn't there. The bed was covered with bits and pieces of costumes—gold lamé shawls, fake-fur stoles, a tricorne sporting a silver cockade. He wondered what Amy was planning to wear, and smiled. She would be a fairy princess in silver tissue, a dewdrop crown atop her small head.

He left the room and continued his search for her. Now he was sorry he hadn't awakened her, because he knew how desperately she wanted them to talk; an entire day had sped by with little contact between them.

Correction, he thought, his body suffusing with warmth, little *recent* contact. The dawn had been filled with touching and murmuring and joining to each other.

He looked for her at dinner, and when she wasn't there either, checked her stateroom again. No luck.

So he finally returned to his suite to dress for the party.

Now he stood before the mirror and tilted his green cap at a rakish angle. His leather jerkin molded his chest and hips, and tights of hunter's green clung to his thighs and calves.

He surveyed his appearance with critical eyes. As an actor, he was used to being appraised rather dispassionately: "Sorry, you're not the right type. Your chest's too big" or "Sorry, there's just something missing. And your eyes are too close together."

Now no one in the film industry found fault with a single inch of him. His chest was *perfect*, his eyes *splendid*. He had become the yardstick against which other aspiring actors were measured. Now everyone was looking for "Derek Morgan" types. Shaking his head at the vagaries of fame, he picked up his crossbow and slung it over his shoulder.

He reached Amy's door and rapped jauntily, eager to see his little princess, nervous about the discussion they must inevitably have.

"Come in," Amy called.

He did, and froze at the jamb. For a moment, he stood speechless. Then he found his voice, and rasped out, "My heaven, you're beautiful."

Before him stood a thirties Cleopatra, bare, beguiling, incredibly sensual. This was not the sunny Amy he knew, the charmer, the giggling sprite. This was a dark temptress who exuded pure sexuality as she stood before him in a plunging cloth-of-gold bra top and a clinging gold skirt slung low on her hips. A train of the same fabric fanned behind her, accentuating her hips even as the spangled brassiere drew his eyes to her cleavage, which she had dusted with gold powder.

A heavy black wig of coiled tresses covered her hair, the ends beaded in gold and turquoise. Beneath the corkscrew bangs, black kohl outlined Amy's huge amber eyes and turquoise covered her lids. Her mouth was blood-red, her skin alabaster. Slave bands at her arms and wrists added to her air of primitive grandeur.

She was a vision from another age, sparkling like a queen, a huge jewel in her navel and bells on the hem of her skirt that tinkled when she took a step forward. And another step, and another . . . and she smelled of patchouli and sandalwood, of sultry nights spent making love on a barge while Nubian slaves rowed the two of them down the banks of the Nile . . .

. . . and the Queen of Love was coming for him, to demand his loyalty, his love, his soul.

"Well?" she asked. Even her voice sounded different—huskier, more sensual, lacking the crystalline sweetness he cherished.

He swallowed hard. Did he know this woman at all, this woman who was to be his wife? He thought back to the many guises he'd seen her in: her Erte gown, her thirties outfits, her jeans. Nothing had prepared him for the woman who stood before him now, so close, he could feel the warmth of her breath on his chest.

He tried to think of something clever to say, some sassy, flirtatious remark that would crack the spell she was weaving around him. He was drowning in her eyes, gasping for breath, and he felt a twinge of . . . what was it, fear? Complete fascination. Obsession. With a pang he understood men who died for their women—for Paris, who launched his fleet for Helen of Troy; for Marc Antony, who turned his back on an empire to fulfill the whims of the imperious Cleopatra herself.

"You . . . have unmanned me," he said finally.

Amy smiled, her ruby lips moist and inviting. "That was hardly my intent."

"Sweeting, I can't believe it's you. Even your voice is different."

She raised her head. "But it's still me."

"Yes," Derek answered, "but who *are* you?"

For a moment she wavered, then sank onto her bed. "You see?" she asked shrilly. "We hardly know each other!"

"Love?" He sat down next to her and took her hand. "Amy, what's wrong?"

Her eyes glistened with unshed tears. "Derek, we have no business getting married! We're both living in a dream world! I have an important job waiting for me, one that could make my name in costume research. You have movies to make. This is the time of our life when we should concentrate on our careers. Don't you see? We'll disappoint everybody if we just drop everything!"

Derek put his arms around her. She was trembling like a hummingbird. "What you mean is, you'll disappoint your big sister if you don't take that job. Did it occur to you that she might be happy for you?"

Amy laughed shortly. "Are you kidding? This is just like something I'd do—I almost flunked out of my first year at San Diego State because I was absolutely infatuated with someone. If Claire hadn't set me straight and told me there'd be no more money for school if I *did* flunk, I might have ruined my college career."

She raised stricken eyes to him. "What kind of life will we have together? Will I stay in London and wait for you, or follow you all over the world?"

Derek shifted uncomfortably. "I was rather hoping you'd come with me, love."

"And do what? Darn your socks? I'll be useless! I'll have wasted myself!"

Though Derek understood what she was saying, her words hurt. Was it wasting herself to love him? How could she consider herself useless when he needed her more than anything in the world?

But still, she was right. It would be difficult for her to find a creative outlet, with the nomadic life he led.

"Well, then, I suppose I'll have to become a university professor," he quipped.

"Don't joke."

He squeezed her shoulder and kissed her cheek, despairing when he felt her stiffen. He hadn't realized that beneath her warm and loving nature was a backbone of iron.

"I'm not joking. Any university in the nation would welcome me as a guest lecturer. Or perhaps the Royal Academy would take me on. There are endless possibilities, love."

He sensed her confusion and wished somehow his kisses could dissolve her fears. He was sorry he hadn't realized how important her job was to her—or perhaps it was what the job symbolized that was important: that she was a responsible woman who took life seriously. That she was no longer impetuous enough to take wild risks and forsake everything for an adventure.

"I was thinking of one of those possibilities," Amy said slowly, curling both her hands around one of his. "How about this: I'll work at the university while you shoot your Australian movie, and then I'll join you for a vacation. We could go more slowly. Maybe even live together for a while and see how we get along."

Derek shook his head. "No. We'll break up eventually if we try that. Our relationship needs to be nurtured, not eternally put on hold."

He saw from her expression that she agreed with him. As her mind worked to find a solution, so did his. He couldn't let her go! What would his life be without her?

"Then I'll go with you, but we'll live together instead of marrying."

He paused, considering, but in his heart he knew that wouldn't work either. "There's a certain commitment one has to a marriage," he said carefully, "that one might not have to just living together. When the going gets tough, we have to be there for each other. If we're just living together, it would be too easy to walk out. Besides, I want you to have the security of knowing I belong to you."

He licked his lips. "It won't be easy, Amy. I can't lie to you and tell you we'll float on a cloud all the time. There will be stories about me and other women in the papers, and mobs of women fans who will try to knock you out of the way to fling themselves at me. But we'll be together. We'll build a life. Please. If we go into this without a serious commitment, our love may not survive."

His heart was hammering in his chest by the time he finished speaking. He knew what he was talking about; he just prayed he could convince her.

Amy looked away from him. Her shoulders sagged, making a gap between her breasts and her bra top, and he saw the circles of her nipples, pink as a satin ballerina slipper. His body ached, and his heart pounded. How could he convince her to say yes?

"If you believe we'll drift apart unless we get

married, maybe we'll drift apart anyway," she murmured.

"No, love, no!" he cried.

The door flew open, surprising them both.

A throng of people dressed in costumes stood on the threshold. "Where are the lovebirds?" cried a sheikh, raising a champagne glass. "Come on! The captain's turned the ball into an engagement party."

"Come on!" Someone dressed as a pirate leaped into the room and grabbed Amy's arm. A duchess took Derek's and urged him to his feet.

"We need to be alone," Derek said quietly, not expecting his wishes to be heeded. The smell of champagne was in the air—the revelers had already begun to celebrate their engagement.

"Oh, I'll bet you do!" drawled the pirate, laughing.

In the hall, a champagne cork popped, followed by cheering.

"Let's go!" the sheikh ordered.

"We'll have to talk later," Derek told Amy.

Amy wouldn't look at him. "I'm not sure there's anything more to say."

She allowed the pirate to lead her away.

Ten

Amy and Derek were herded by their tipsy, cheering escorts to the Grand Salon, where the costume ball was being held. The Salon was an even more stunning place than the dining room, the walls crowded with gleaming lacquerwork and mosaics done in early Deco style. On either side of the towering doors posed statues of white marble satyrs holding frond-shaped lamps, sloe eyes blank, bodies sinuous and erotic.

"Here they are!" the pirate announced, raising Amy's arm.

At once everyone in the glittering room turned and applauded. Puffs of confetti mushroomed above the heads of kings and damsels, a monk or two, several cancan girls, and the captain, splendid in his dress whites.

Amy saw that silver and white wedding decorations had hastily been added to the elegant decor: silver bells above the doorways, festoons of white and silver on the refreshment tables. An ice sculpture had been moved off-center, and in its place stood a tiered cake frosted in ice blue and white.

The captain made his way through the crowd,

shook Derek's hand, kissed Amy's cheek, and led them into the room.

"My best wishes to you both," he said, beaming like a pleased father. He motioned to the band, which at once began to play the "Blue Danube."

Amy swallowed as Derek took her into his arms, needing to keep her distance from him in order to think straight, unable not to thaw in his embrace as he glided in the elegant waltz pattern.

"I rather guess this is destined to be our song," he said quietly.

When she didn't answer, Derek's face fell with disappointment.

The music swelled and grew around them, lush, cavalier, ripe with the promise of romance. A fairy-tale melody for a fairy-tale story. Love, true love, in the arms of the world's most desirable man . . .

"Your hand is clammy," Derek said. "You're trembling."

"We shouldn't do it, Derek. It's crazy."

"*Not* doing it is crazier. Amy, you know that job's not for you! Can't you trust life enough to know you don't have to give me up to fulfill yourself?"

Without realizing what she was doing, she clung to him. "Derek, can't we just live together?"

"You know that won't work. I saw in your eyes that you know it. Besides, I want to be married. I want all the trappings, social, legal, and spiritual. I want my mum to call you "Daughter Amy" and teach you how to make leeks like a proper Welsh wife."

"She might not like me."

"She will adore you. As I do." He focused the force of his eyes on her. "Amy, I need the commitment of marriage."

The waltz faded and a rhythmic rock beat swelled beneath the applause as other couples took the floor. A man tapped Derek on the shoulder, asking to cut in, and Derek reluctantly relinquished Amy to him.

After that man came another, and another, and soon almost an hour passed without Amy and Derek speaking.

And then yet another man cut in. He was English, and dressed as a knight.

"My best wishes to you," he said as they began to dance.

"Thank you," she replied, forcing the smile plastered on her face to stay for yet another dance, another hour, until she could find Derek again.

They chatted for a few minutes—about the cruise, about England, about Derek, and then the man dropped a bomb that shattered the last illusions Amy had about her fantasy of true, perfect love.

"You know, I've dated Derek's ex-wife a few times. She's quite lovely."

Amy froze. A chill swept from her feet to her head, submerging her into ice water as she stopped dancing and gaped at the man. "His . . . *what?*"

He looked taken aback. "Oh, dear, have I said something gauche? I suppose it was rude of me to mention her at your engagement party. I am sorry."

His words swam inside her head. She heard them as if he were speaking in slow motion. They made no sense and yet they pierced her heart. "He's . . . been married before?"

The man grimaced. "You didn't know. Looks like I've put my foot in it, doesn't it?"

"I—I—"

He gave her his arm. "I think we'd better leave the floor. You're chalk-white."

Numb, Amy allowed herself to lean on the man for support. She had almost forgotten how to walk, and it seemed to take forever to weave their way past the gyrating couples who were smiling at her.

"May I get you a drink?" the knight asked as they neared the bar, but Amy shook her head.

"No, thanks. I—I need to get out of here."

"Let's get some air." The man gestured toward the doors.

She touched his arm. "Thank you, but I need to be alone."

"I'm really awfully sorry. I feel like such an idiot."

Her throat ached, but somehow she managed to rasp out an empty reassurance. "No, it's all right. I'm glad you told me, so please don't feel guilty about it."

The man shrugged. "It's not as if he's married now, you know."

Amy nodded grimly. "Yes, I know. Thank you again."

He withdrew as she swept out of the room and rushed outside.

The night was brisk, but not too cold. The moon was a disk of pale silver like a jewel in an Egyptian headdress, and tears of silver stars sprang to Amy's eyes as she remembered Derek's reaction to her appearance. She had been new to him, a surprise.

Where did the surprises end? Why hadn't he told her he was married? Why did she have to hear about it from a complete stranger? Why had he insisted that marriage was some kind of safety net beneath the wild trapeze flight they were contemplating? Obviously the net hadn't broken his fall the first time he had taken a wife.

The first time. If he had prepared her, she could have handled the pangs that now assailed her. He had already done all the things she'd thought they might experience for the first time together—the exchanging of vows and rings, the bridal clothes, the scent of flowers everywhere. The jitters of the night before, the hopes and dreams that danced on your face as the organ played "Here Comes the Bride."

The tears were streams of silver on her cheeks. How many other secrets had he kept locked inside? Did he have any children? Did he still love his former wife?

Why hadn't he told her?

"Ah, there you are!" The captain chortled behind her. "Come back in. We're toasting both our brides and grooms!"

"Both . . . ?" Amy murmured, not able to summon the strength to escape the firm grasp of the captain's hand below her elbow.

The doors flew open. Hastily she wiped her face with the back of her hand, squinting at the lights and smiling faces as if they were too bright for her eyes.

Her hand came away with eye makeup on it, and she realized her crying had ravaged her face. "One moment," she whispered. "I need to—"

"Here we are!" The captain's voice boomed as he led her to the table where the tiered cake sat in state.

The Bordons and Derek were already gathered there. When the captain proudly presented Amy to her fiancé, Derek quickly produced a handkerchief and handed it to her. His face was lined with concern. He murmured, "Ah, love, don't fret so," as Amy daubed the streaked kohl and turquoise powder from beneath her eyes.

"Derek, you . . . didn't . . . " *tell me*, she wanted to say, but knew she couldn't say anything more or she would break down in front of everyone.

The ship's photographer bent in front of the table, and the cruise director handed both Amy and Mrs. Bordon a knife. "Now, gentlemen, put your hand over your lady's, and we'll cut on the count of three," the photographer directed.

No, no, Amy pleaded silently. Her heart was thudding violently, and Derek glanced down at her worriedly as the flashbulb blinded them.

"Now, a glass of champagne for each of them!" The cruise director quickly complied.

Amy accepted her goblet, mechanically toasting Derek and the Bordons, resigned to the fact that she must go through the motions or cause a scene in front of the entire ship. She tried to smile as best she could, remembering that these would be pictures the Bordons would treasure. Tomorrow night they would renew their vows in the ship's chapel, and Mrs. Bordon would be a bride once more. . . .

As they drank the champagne, stewards quickly moved in to cut the cake and distribute pieces to the guests. Then vigorous music pulsated through the room, and attention was taken off the two couples.

"That was so sweet of you, Captain," Mrs. Bordon sang as she downed her champagne. "Wasn't it, Bobo, dear?"

"Yes, indeed, my darling."

Mrs. Bordon regarded her husband with such intense adoration that Amy squirmed behind her haze of agony. After what Mrs. Bordon had revealed about Mr. Bordon's unfaithfulness, how could she look at him like that?

"We're going to have a private little cocktail party before the wedding tomorrow," Mrs. Bordon went on. "I do hope you can attend, Captain. And the two of you, of course." With a wave of her hand she included Derek and Amy.

"Thank you, we'd love to," Derek said, placing a hand on Amy's shoulder. The weight, once cherished, was a heavy burden to her, and she moved uneasily away.

"I'd be happy to attend," the captain added. His eyes twinkled. "I'm glad my last voyage on the *Meg* is ending with such happiness. There's nothing I like better than shipboard weddings." The captain looked pointedly at Derek, then at Amy.

All eyes were on Amy' awaiting her reaction,

"I . . . I . . . excuse me," she murmured wretchedly, and rushed out of the room.

Though she ran as fast as she could, Derek caught up with her just outside the doors.

"Let me go!" She sobbed as he grabbed her hand.

"Amy, what's wrong? This is more than just mere nerves!" he insisted, his voice low and husky.

When she didn't reply, he wrapped his arms around her as if he were shielding her from the rain and walked farther away from the ballroom. "Darling, please. Talk to me."

She tried to speak, and failed. Licking her lips, she shook her head. "Can't."

"Sweeting." He kissed her hands. "Trust me enough to tell me. Whatever it is, I'll put it right."

"It's too late for that!" she cried out, then looked around to see if anyone else had heard her. But the passageway they had wandered down was deserted; everyone was at the party.

He cocked his head. "What do you mean?"

She lowered her gaze to his Robin Hood boots. "You should've told me," she whispered. "Why didn't you?" She looked at him. "Why didn't you tell me you'd been married before?" At his look of shock, she pressed on. "First you didn't tell me you were leaving two days after we landed. Then you went on and on and *on* about what a difference being married would make to our relationship, and you didn't even tell me!"

Her hands flew to her face, and she wept bitterly, too weakened by her confusion to fight when Derek pulled her against his chest and rocked her.

"I'm sorry, love. I was going to. I really was. But I supposed we'd talk more after the party, and I would've told you then." He sighed. "It seems someone is always beating me to the punch, first Mara, and now—who told you I'd been married before? It's not common knowledge."

"Some man who's dated her," she managed to get out.

"Damn him," Derek said fiercely.

"Damn him?" Amy reared out of his embrace. "I'm grateful to him! I'd probably never have known if he hadn't told me!"

Derek's eyes flashed. "That's not true! I already said I was going to tell you!"

"And do you think I believe you anymore? Do you think I'd trust you after this?"

"Amy—" He reached out for her.

"Don't! Don't touch me! Just leave me alone!"

She turned and ran wildly, not knowing where she was going, not caring. She heard Derek shouting, "Amy! I love you! I love you! Please come back!"

"Never," she whispered to herself as the bond between them pulled at her, its power straining to wrench her back to him. It was like a living thing, and she almost heard it wailing in sorrow as she hurtled down the passageway, each step adding power to the decision that was forming in her mind. . . .

Where would she run?

To a boring job that had never appealed to her in the first place, she admitted. She had accepted it to prove to her sister that she was a responsible adult.

To a lonely life as she struggled to get over Derek, to forget his smile, his touch, his love . . .

"Oh, what am I doing? Why am I doing it?" she cried aloud.

She wandered the ship, half-hoping, half-dreading, that Derek would seek her out. But she was alone with her fear and confusion.

Alone with her choices.

She leaned over the railing and watched the water rush by, Cleopatra on her barge, feeling lost, wishing Claire were there to tell her what to do.

But no, the days of her big sister's protection were over. She must make her way in the world, and do a good job of it, too, as Claire had. Claire, always the dependable one, the substitute for the mother Amy couldn't remember, the buffer between her and Aunt Norma. Amy's first knight in shining armor, in a way.

But Claire had married. She had forsaken their life on the road to find love.

Ah, yes, but both of them had since admitted that traveling with the Renaissance troupe had been a way to escape from problems, not to solve them. Claire had faced life head on when she became a married woman.

Disheartened, Amy meandered aimlessly through the ship, coming to a rest at last in front of the door to the Bordons' suite. Timidly, she knocked.

Mrs. Bordon herself answered. "Oh, my poor baby!" she said, throwing her arms around Amy and leading her into the suite. She was dressed in a powder-blue velour bathrobe. "Come in. Sit down. Your arms are frozen!"

"It was colder than I thought," Amy murmured, touching her own chilled skin. "Thank you," she added when Mrs. Bordon handed her a glass of brandy.

"Bobo's gone out. We're alone," Mrs. Bordon told her, sitting beside her on their enormous bed. The room was filled with bouquets of tea roses and baby's breath.

"Has something happened?" she asked kindly.

Amy fought back fresh tears. "I'm just so confused! Every time I turn around, something new comes up!" She sipped the brandy. "He's been married before!"

Mrs. Bordon waited. When Amy said nothing more, a gentle smile played on her lips, and she touched Amy's cheek. "My dear, most people his age usually have been married before. Divorce doesn't carry the stigma it did in my day."

"But he didn't tell me! I suggested we live together and—"

"You did?" Mrs. Bordon asked, appearing slightly shocked.

"But he wouldn't hear of it. He kept talking about how we needed the commitment of marriage to help us through the hard times, and—"

"And he's quite right." Now Mrs. Bordon smiled broadly. "This changes my opinion of your marriage entirely. If he has that much sense—and honor—then I'd advise you not to let him get away. Any man who would rather marry than . . . keep company, especially if he's already been married, is a man who knows exactly what he's doing."

Puzzled, Amy frowned, even as her heart leaped with hope. "You really think so?"

"Well, consider it, dear. Would you rather have some starry-eyed boy who has no idea what he's letting himself in for, or a grown man with a little seasoning?"

Amy's pulse quickened. Forcing herself to play devil's advocate, she pointed out, "But he didn't tell me."

"Perhaps he was afraid to."

Amy bit her lower lip. "Actually, he said he was planning to tell me. The man I danced with beat him to it."

"There, you see?" Mrs. Bordon poured Amy another glass of brandy and helped herself to one as well. "He had good intentions."

"You sound like you're defending him. Only this morning, you disapproved of the whole idea of our marrying."

Mrs. Bordon made a face. "I did, didn't I? Perhaps I was projecting my own fears. You know, I assumed renewing my vows with Bobo would mean simply mouthing the words. But after you've lived with someone for over fifty years and you know all his flaws, it's important to be able to say honestly that you'd do it all again."

Her face grew rosy and her eyes moist. "And after considering it, yes, I would marry my darling Bobo all over again. Indiscretions and all. I love him that much."

She brushed Amy's hand with her own, the wrinkled, blue-veined flesh of experience touching smooth, untried youth and impatience.

"Derek hasn't set you an easy task, deciding this fast, but I suspect you know in your heart what the right decision is."

Amy held the older woman's hand. They sat together for a few moments, smiling at each other, and then they both burst into happy tears.

"Let's make it a double ceremony. You'll be such a lovely bride!" Mrs. Bordon said, embracing Amy. "You must alter my gown and wear it tomorrow night. And we'll—"

"Oh, no, I couldn't do that!" Amy insisted. "Besides, tomorrow night's *your* wedding. I don't want to take away from it."

"Nonsense. Bobo and I insist. In fact, we won't get married unless *you* do." She tilted her head. "You're a very dear girl. It would have been such a joy to me to have had children. What I wouldn't have given for a daughter like you."

She looped an errant curl behind Amy's ear. "Go find him, Amy. I'm sure his poor heart is breaking. And make him happy, dear." She hugged Amy tightly. "Make him so very happy."

Amy searched for Derek everywhere, receiving a few strange looks as she rushed about in her

Cleopatra outfit. She tried his stateroom, the bars, the Salon, but he was nowhere to be found.

Then she stood still and closed her eyes to think. If she were Derek, where would she go?

She knit her brow as she waited for the answer to come to her. And then she smiled as an idea emerged.

Yes, that was where he would go. And if she knew that about him already, then she knew him well enough to entwine her life with his.

She returned to her stateroom and pulled on her coat over her costume. Then she tiptoed down the corridor that led to the ship's chapel and quietly pushed the door open.

Derek was kneeling in the front pew, hands clasped, head bowed.

"Oh, my darling," she whispered, and walked down the aisle to his side.

Hushed electric light from behind a stained-glass window brushed the crown of his head with a rainbow of muted color. She watched the colors shift as she drew nearer, her heart rushing, her breath stopping as she heard him pray.

"Please, Lord," he said with all his being, resting his forehead on his clenched hands. *"Please."*

"Derek." Amy touched his shoulder and he jerked, galvanized.

She caught her breath when he turned around. Never had she seen such hopeful joy on the face of another person. His skin glowed as if a flame burned inside him, and his eyes shone golden and loving as he saw her.

Still kneeling, he caught her hand in his and kissed it. He kept his head lowered for an instant, and when he looked back up, there were tears in his eyes.

"We'll be married," Amy said tenderly. "It's what I want. I know that now. And I'm not afraid, my darling. Not anymore."

Derek sagged with relief. "My prayers are answered then."

She brushed his cheek with her fingertips. "Mine too. Derek, forgive me for ever doubting you."

"Let me tell you about my first marriage," he said in a rush.

"No. You don't need to. I trust you."

"But you deserve to know. She was a society girl and I was still struggling." He smiled wanly. "Still starving. She just grew tired of waiting for my success."

"Shh, love, It doesn't matter."

"I was young; we both were. We didn't know what love was." He caught her hand and kissed it reverently. "But I do now."

"And I know." She knelt beside him. "I was so afraid to love you. It seemed like something bad would have to happen to cancel out the good. That happened a lot when I was little, so I'd make things up to comfort myself. I pretended too much. I wanted life to be happier than it was. . . ."

"I know. I understand. It was that way for me too. But Amy, together we can forget the sad memories. We can make new ones, good ones."

"Yes, Derek, my love. Yes."

He closed his eyes. "Smell the lavender?"

"Aye, king of my heart. And I feel the warm breeze of summer." She held out her arms. "Come dance with me among the heather. Dance with your Queen of Love."

Derek glanced at the altar, smiled, and then rose. "Our life will be nothing but waltzes, my darling."

She laid her head on his shoulder as they walked up the aisle toward the back of the chapel. "I know, Derek. I can hear the music."

*   *   *

As a concession to Derek and Amy's wedding, Loretta Hansen moved the International Society of Mystery Fans accusation party from midnight of the last night to early in the afternoon to give them plenty of time to prepare.

Derek and Amy strode boldly down the corridor to where the fans had assembled, Derek in his black turtleneck, jeans, and sneakers, with the addition of a jaunty tweed cap slung low over his eyes. Amy wore clothes she had thrown together for the occasion: a refitted dress of Mara's—a scarlet sheath with a scooped neckline—and a red hat with a black polka-dot veil. When Derek saw her, he looked taken aback for a moment, then remarked, "I dreamed of you in that outfit. We were going to steal the crown jewels."

She laughed merrily. " 'Ow about them next, mate?" she asked in a terrible Cockney accent.

He slid an arm around her waist. "I've got the jewel I want. Having you makes me the richest man alive."

"Oh, Derek," she said, sighing. "In five hours we'll be married."

"Yes, love."

They kissed as they waited behind the closed door, listening to Loretta conducting the accusations. Each member of the group had to state whom he thought the thief was, and why.

"I know precisely who it is, my dears," trilled a familiar voice. "And I know who helped him! Derek and Amy Morgan!"

"Oh, Geneva," Derek said in mock exasperation. "That Swiss cow!"

"You're right, Mrs. Bordon. And here they are now!"

Loretta opened the door and grinned at the kissing couple. "Jig's up, folks. Come in and take a bow."

To the eruption of laughter and applause, Derek

and Amy strode into the lounge. Amy grinned at Mrs. Bordon and shook her head.

"Technically, you're wrong. I'm not Amy Morgan *yet*. But how did you guess?"

"I'm smart for an old woman. Still, what clinched it was the fan. It made me think of someone who would have fans. A movie star!"

"Right you were," Derek said drolly. "You gave us a run for our money when you stole the loot."

Mrs. Bordon preened. "I did, didn't I? And I tried to inject a little more suspense into the proceedings by pretending to be robbed. Unfortunately, my niece saw my bracelet under the chair." She laughed. "The captain was in on it, of course. He was so disappointed he didn't get to play his part!"

"You should take up acting," Derek said teasingly.

"Perhaps I will. Well, please present me with my trophy and I'll be off. I have a wedding to attend this evening."

"Of course, Mrs. Bordon. At your command."

Derek handed her a huge gold trophy topped with an old-fashioned magnifying glass and Sherlock Holmes cap. "To the master sleuth among us, the queen of detectives, the peerless Geneva Bordon." He pecked her cheek.

Laughing, she kissed him back. "Ah, it's like the old days all over again." She smiled dreamily at Amy. "Just like Errol Flynn."

Derek and Amy lingered for a few minutes after Mrs. Bordon left, then made their own excuses and took their leave.

As Derek walked Amy back to her stateroom to change for the prenuptial cocktail party, he asked, "Why the devil do you two keep talking about Errol Flynn?"

She grinned at him. "Because he was too good to be true."

"What?"

She opened the door and waved at him. "I'll tell you about it sometime."

Then, laughing happily, she shut the door in his face.

At seven forty-five that evening, the wedding guests began to fill the pews of the ship's chapel. The tone of the gathering was formal and elegant. The ladies were exquisitely attired in floor-length damasks originally designed by Schiaparelli and printed taffetas and soufflés cut on the bias; and long white gloves made their arms graceful as swans' necks. The gloves of the ushers set off their full-dress tailcoats as they guided the ladies to their seats, husbands or escorts following behind. People spoke in hushed, excited voices as the organist played "Maytime," the "Blue Danube," an Elizabethan tarantella, and other pieces, in a medley of the Bordons' and Derek's and Amy's favorites.

Mr. Bordon and Derek both appeared next to the captain, who would be performing the ceremony. From her vantage point behind the door, Amy noted with jittery good humor that Mr. Bordon looked more nervous than Derek, whose radiant joy filled the chapel.

She also noticed that Mara was seated beside Giovanni, gazing at him with a look of rapture. Amy found it in her heart to wish Mara luck in love at last, and to hope that the two of them might find the happiness she had found with Derek.

At precisely eight o'clock, the triumphal first bars of the "Wedding March" announced the procession of the two brides.

Amy and Mrs. Bordon walked side by side, Mrs. Bordon in her wedding dress, Amy in her simple ivory satin gown with the bell sleeves. They both carried bouquets of roses and Amy wore a circlet of them in her hair, which was swept into a glowing cascade of Grecian curls.

Everyone stood to honor them, and down the aisle Amy floated, regal as a queen, impatient to reach the side of her beloved.

The two couples joined hands before the captain. Derek gazed at Amy with such intense happiness that she had to dab her eyes. When she lifted her gaze back to him, the captain spoke the precious, old words:

"Dearly beloved, we are gathered here . . ."

Oh, Derek, I love you so, she told him soundlessly. And Derek answered back, dipping his head to brush a tear from his eye.

Much later, after the champagne and the rice, after Derek had slid her gown from her body and they made love for the first time as husband and wife; after a night of ecstasy and the shores of England appeared before them in the dawn, Derek rolled over, kissed Amy roundly, and said, "I have a wonderful surprise for you."

She snuggled against him. "You're pregnant," she said.

"No. But I certainly hope you will be, one day."

"How many times?" she asked.

"As many as you like, darling. But that's not my surprise. I got you a job."

She raised herself on her arms. "What? What kind of job?"

"I didn't want to say anything until I was sure. Well, the steward brought me this cable while you were sleeping." He reached over to the nightstand and waved a piece of yellow paper.

He handed it to her. "ALL AS YOU WISH STOP PRESS GOING WILD STOP BEST WISHES STOP GEOFFREY."

"Who's Geoffrey?" Amy asked, studying the note. "And what does all this mean?"

Derek kissed her cheek. "What it means, Mrs. Morgan, is that Mr. Morgan has amended all his contracts. From now on, a prime requisite for my services is the employment of a certain costumer on the set."

When she didn't say anything, Derek kissed her again. "You, Amy. You'll be working on the costumes for my films. That way we'll be together and you'll still have your career."

Amy's heart pounded. A perfect solution! So simple, and yet . . .

And yet it had to be too good to be true.

"Isn't it . . . illegal, or something? What about the unions? I mean, isn't this nepotism, my getting a job because I'm married to you?"

"Geoff's taking care of the legalities and the union membership. As for the nepotism problem, that'll evaporate the moment you get to work. When they see how skilled you are, they'll forget the rest," Derek said confidently.

Amy's mind whirled. Working in the movies! At school, her professors had warned how difficult it was to get into that line of work, so she had never even considered it.

It truly *was* the perfect solution. They could be together, both working and fulfilled. And he was right: Once she showed them what she could do, they would forgive the one act of pulling rank that had brought her into films.

It was too much. Amy began to weep.

At once Derek dropped the cable and pulled her into his arms. "Sweet! What's wrong? I thought this would make you happy!"

She cried against his chest. Life was a fantasy, after all; an eternal daydream. There *were* knights in shining armor—hadn't she married one? And there was such a thing as a perfect ending . . . and a glorious beginning.

"Please, dearest," Derek begged, "tell me why you're crying."

She laid her head against his chest, cherished and protected within the magic circle of their abiding love. "I'm crying because I love you so much," she whispered, gazing up at him. "And because we really are going to live happily ever after."

Derek smiled. "Did you ever doubt it?"

And then he kissed her. And they joined their flesh together, and celebrated a love that would endure forever.

THE EDITOR'S CORNER

As you know from the sneak previews I've been giving in the Editor's Corner, you have some wonderful treats in store—and none better than the four for next month!

We start off with a gloriously intense and touching love story in **CHAR'S WEBB**, LOVESWEPT #151, by Kathleen Downes. The story begins on an astonishing note: Hero Keith Webb has "invented" a fiancée because the young daughter of a friend has a crush on him and he wants to let her down gently. For his lady love he had chosen a first name he'd always liked, Charlotte, and for her last—well, his imagination failed and he had only come up with Smith. Now, just put yourself in Keith's place when the management consulting firm he hired sends out one of their best and brightest employees and *she* introduces herself as—you guessed it!—Charlotte Smith. The real Charlotte is as lovely, sensitive, and tender-hearted as Keith's fantasy fiancée . . . but she's also devoted to her job, has vowed never to mix work and love and—ah, but to say more would give away too much of a vastly entertaining and twisty plot, so I'll only encourage you to anticipate being trapped like Keith in the enchantment of **CHAR'S WEBB**.

If you've just finished **ALWAYS,** my guess is that you feel as though you've been wrung out emotionally. (I certainly felt that way when I read and worked on that marvelous love story!) Now, for next month, Iris Johansen greatly changes pace with **EVERLASTING,** LOVESWEPT #152, in which she gives you a romp of a romance. Oh, it is intensely emotional, too, of course, but it *is* also a true "Johansen romp." You met Kira Rubinoff in **ALWAYS** and may have leaped to the correct conclusion that she was your next heroine. In **EVERLASTING** she is off to America for help to rescue her beloved Marna . . . and

continued

that help is in the form of one Zack Damon, powerful industrialist, famed lover, part American Indian and proud of his heritage—in short, just one heck of a hero. Now for the romp part: there are gypsies and dungeons, palaces, plots, magic, and kings. And there is grand, glorious, passionate romantic love between Kira and Zack. Iris simply keeps coming up with one lovely romance after another, and aren't we lucky?

Our other two authors for the month—the much loved Miz Pickart and Miz Brown—have just as wonderful and fertile imaginations. First, you'll enjoy Joan's charming **MISTER LONELYHEARTS**, LOVESWEPT #153. The title refers to the hero's occupation: he writes a newspaper advice column, focusing primarily on love and romance. Heroine Chapel Barclay is a lawyer—and a lady who is as mad as a wet hen at the "Dear Ben" column and the blasted man who writes it! She thinks the advice he gives out is garbage, pure and simple, that it's destructive to creating real and lasting relationships. When they confront one another on a television talk show, Ben is the overwhelming winner of their debate . . . and later full of remorse that the lovely Chapel had suffered from his remarks, even though he'd softened them because of her remarkable effect on him. But if Ben and Chapel had thought sparks had flown between them on that telecast, did they have a surprise ahead. When he sought her out to apologize, it was the beginning of a physical and emotional conflagration that made the great Chicago blaze look like a small campfire! Another memorable winner from Joan Elliott Pickart.

Sandra Brown's stunningly beautiful contribution to your reading enjoyment next month is **22 INDIGO PLACE**, LOVESWEPT #154. A romance of conflict and drama and sensuality, **22 INDIGO PLACE** is aptly titled, since the house at this address has played such an important role throughout the lives of the heroine and hero that it

continued

almost becomes a living, vivid character in the story. And the story of James Paden and Laura Nolan is breathtaking. James was the high school "bad boy"—complete with motorcycle, black leather jacket, and shades. Laura was "Miss Goody Two-Shoes." Their contacts back then were brief yet fierce, and when they meet again their impact on one another is just as dramatic. But now, added to James's devastating sensual power over Laura, is his economic power. How he wields it and witholds it makes for one of Sandra Brown's best ever love stories.

We hope you enjoy these four LOVESWEPTs as much as everyone here in the office did.

Warm good wishes,

Sincerely,

Carolyn Nichols

Carolyn Nichols
   Editor
LOVESWEPT
Bantam Books, Inc.
666 Fifth Avenue
New York, NY 10103

LOVESWEPT

Love Stories you'll never forget
by authors you'll always remember

☐	21753	**Stubborn Cinderalla #135** Eugenia Riley	$2.50
☐	21746	**The Rana Look #136** Sandra Brown	$2.50
☐	21750	**Tarnished Armor #137** Peggy Webb	$2.50
☐	21757	**The Eagle Catcher #138** Joan Elliott Pickart	$2.50
☐	21755	**Delilah's Weakness #139** Kathleen Creighton	$2.50
☐	21758	**Fire In The Rain #140** Fayrene Preston	$2.50
☐	21759	**Crescendo #141** A. Staff & S. Goldenbaum	$2.50
☐	21754	**Trouble In Triplicate #142** Barbara Boswell	$2.50

Prices and availability subject to change without notice.

Buy them at your local bookstore or use this handy coupon for ordering:

Bantam Books, Inc., Dept. SW2, 414 East Golf Road, Des Plaines, Ill. 60016

Please send me the books I have checked above. I am enclosing $_____
(please add $1.50 to cover postage and handling). Send check or money order
—no cash or C.O.D.'s please.

Mr/Mrs/Miss _____

Address _____

City _____ State/Zip _____

SW2—7/86

Please allow four to six weeks for delivery. This offer expires 1/87.

LOVESWEPT

Love Stories you'll never forget by authors you'll always remember

☐	21760	**Donovan's Angel #143** Peggy Webb	$2.50
☐	21761	**Wild Blue Yonder #144** Millie Grey	$2.50
☐	21762	**All Is Fair . . . #145** Linda Cajio	$2.50
☐	21763	**Journey's End #146** Joan Elliott Pickart	$2.50
☐	21751	**Once In Love With Amy #147** Nancy Holder	$2.50
☐	21749	**Always #148** Iris Johansen	$2.50
☐	21765	**Time After Time #149** Kay Hooper	$2.50
☐	21767	**Hot Tamales #150** Sara Orwig	$2.50

Prices and availability subject to change without notice.

Buy them at your local bookstore or use this handy coupon for ordering:

Bantam Books, Inc., Dept. SW3, 414 East Golf Road, Des Plaines, Ill. 60016

Please send me the books I have checked above. I am enclosing $_____
(please add $1.50 to cover postage and handling). Send check or money order
—no cash or C.O.D.'s please.

Mr/Mrs/Miss _____

Address _____

City _____ State/Zip _____

SW3—7/86
Please allow four to six weeks for delivery. This offer expires 1/87.